THE GOOD MAN

THE GOOD MAN

THE COMPANY FILES: 1

GABRIEL VALJAN

A Note on the Text

The Good Man, the first in The Company Files series appeared in 2017. When the rights reverted to me, I trimmed the word count to increase the pace and I expanded on some of the dialog. Everything else remains intact.

Praise for The Good Man

"Set in post-war Vienna, with dialogue as smart and snappy as Chandler's, and a plot as intriguing as le Carré's, Gabriel Valjan brings us *The Good Man*, a Cold War novel about unlikely alliances and unusual bedfellows. In a Europe turned upside down in the aftermath of World War II, we enter a world of grays—where black and white is dangerous thinking, where good and bad are not easily recognized or reconciled. I can't wait for the next installment of The Company Files!"—Tina deBellegarde, author of the Agatha-nominated Batavia-on-Hudson series

Chapter One

Nothing good comes from a call in the middle of the night.

At 0300 his little black beauty warbled from the nightstand, and stirred Walker from an erotic embrace of his pillow. Grable, his .45, slept next to the receiver. She could sleep through anything. He was jealous as he fumbled for the phone.

"Awake?" Jack's distinctive voice came over the wire.

"I am now." Walker's eyes focused on becoming alert.

"Meet me at the Narrenturm, ninth district."

"Why?"

"The IP are here already."

Walker washed a hand over his face, still in the fog. "What is it, Jack?"

"Dead body in the Fruitcake House."

The informative sentence ended with a click. The IP, the International Police, was a guarantee that the crime scene would not be kept contained.

Walker threw his legs over the side of the bed.

His room was square, clean, and impersonal. There was no pretension to domesticity, like paintings, books, or excess furniture. The room measured 50 square meters. His bed was the bedroom, the upholstered chair, his living room, and a hot plate for his kitchen. A walnut armoire rested against the wall, next to the bathroom door. There were doors to a balcony so small that it would make suicide difficult.

Each night before bed Walker draped a towel over the chair, and he placed a pail of water on his balcony. Then he'd inventory the room. He would know if something was moved in the monastic cell that he called home.

Out of habit he slept barefoot, his feet in the open air, so he could sense if someone had entered the apartment.

He dropped his shorts, went out onto the balcony naked in the cold air, picked up the pail of now freezing water and poured it over his head.

He had learned this trick from a Russian POW. Cold water forced the body to discharge negativity and disease. The same POW, he was told through a translator, did this ritual every single day without fail regardless of season. Walker never got used to the shock. The water made his skin scream. Any heaviness escaped him through his heels and his mind focused. He was awake, ready for whatever Jack Marshall had for him at the insane asylum.

He toweled off, dressed, and coaxed Grable out of her sleep and under his arm.

* * *

The Narrenturm sat next to the Allgemeines Krankenhaus, the largest hospital in Austria. The first lightning rods in Vienna were installed on the roof, and this institution was where blood groups were first typed. The Narrenturm was the second mental hospital in Europe after Bedlam in London. The German word for the place was Gugelhupf for its architecture, which was why Jack called it 'Fruitcake.' Like the dessert Jack had referenced, the building had a corkscrew circular corridor and twenty-eight patient rooms on each of its five floors. Each room displayed a slit window that only a starving bird could contemplate for roosting. Escaping the place was as formidable as finding it.

The local Viennese called the place 'The Fool's Tower' because the psychiatric hospital has housed the mentally ill, the criminally insane, and political prisoners. Patients, chained to lattice doors, screamed like unrepentant heretics in medieval dungeons well into the nineteenth century.

* * *

After Walker flashed his papers and asked for directions, the MP told him in factual German that Courtyard 6 was accessible from one of several entrances. 'Take Alserstrasse, Garnisongasse, or Spitalgasse, and then consult the map.' It was just the right amount of sibilants and consonants in German to confuse him.

In darkness and frustration Walker found the wrought-iron gate with the curved snake. He ran his fingers over the Rod of Asclepius, the diamond-shaped iron fixtures for snakeskin. Old man Hermes must have taken back one of his snakes. The Caduceus of Hermes, he remembered, had two serpents.

He climbed steps, heard voices above him in the darkness. He saw Jack, some members of the International Police around him, the air charged with a Babel of languages. Even in a crowd Jack Marshall stood out as a man not to crowd.

Hands behind his back, Jack whispered to Walker. "The German word for magician is Der Zauberer. Whoever did this is a magician. He performed his trick, and then poof, gone."

Approaching them were the four policemen, one representative for each of the countries that controlled the city. They reported to an Inspector, each in their respective languages. Walker knew the Inspector would summarize the scene for him and Jack in English.

The French IP, with the long haggard face from smoking too many cigarettes, spoke with a phlegmatic bass. The Brit talked details in a reedy voice and posh accent. The Russian, after he had spoken, stood at attention, winter in his face, whereas the American, a young kid, gave a report, about as graceful as a southpaw in a room of righties. Walker's ears listened for any German, keen for the second verb at the end of the sentence so he could understand what was being said. The Inspector scribbled notes with a very short pencil that took brevity to an art form.

In a lilting Austrian-inflected English, he said, "Gentlemen, it appears we have an unfortunate scenario here. The victim was discovered two hours ago. The IP arrived at the scene after hearing a tip from an informant who said this facility was being used for illegal activities. Thinking that they might discover black-market penicillin or some other commodities popular these days, the IP found the body. A medical examiner is with the deceased as I speak."

The man continued as the four policemen lingered behind him.

"The victim in question *was*, according to our preliminary findings, a man of the medical profession with questionable ethics."

Jack, hearing the euphemism, said, "You mean a Nazi doctor."

The Frenchman behind the Inspector coughed, "Bosch."

The Inspector's eyes acknowledged the profanity without turning his head. "The deceased is said to have performed medical experiments on prisoners in the camps. He did horrible things to children, women, and particularly, Russian prisoners of war. Unconscionable."

The Russian, a silent Ivan, stared ahead without a flinch.

The Inspector with a modest bow of the head and genteel click of his heels handed Jack a piece of paper. "It's all there," he said. Jack said nothing, accepted the paper and began the short walk to the scene.

Jack and Walker entered the patient's cell. The room smelled of something tarry. Some other men there left in whispers, leaving them alone with the doctor and the corpse.

"How's the patient?" Jack asked the man.

"Dead a day or two according to his liver temperature. Rigor has set, as you well can see from the positioning." The doctor made his own notes while he talked.

"Any thoughts to cause of death, Herr Doktor?" Walker asked.

The doctor used his fingers to show an invisible syringe and did the motion of pressing the plunger. Abgespritzt. Lethal injection. I would say, carbolic acid."

"Sounds to me that would be a fast way to go, Doctor," Jack said.

"Not necessarily. Ten to fifteen millimeters of the liquid, if injected directly into the heart, should induce ventricular tachycardia in, say, fifteen seconds. Our man here was not so lucky. First, I found no such puncture in the chest. I did find, however, a puncture in his arm. I would say this man took an hour to die." With this pronouncement, the small birdlike man clicked his little black bag shut and left Jack and Walker inside the cell.

Walker imagined the history within the room. He estimated that the chamber was tall enough, walls thick enough, that a man could scream all he wanted and nobody would know he existed. He imagined centuries of torment within the cell and maybe some claw marks on the walls, too. "How did he get in here?"

"And what does the way the body was staged mean?" Jack asked.

The dead man had been propped up on a stool meant for prisoners, naked. A metal T behind him formed a cross bar. His left arm was secure to iron while his right hand was placed over his heart. The elbow of the left arm displayed the injection site. The head was cocked back, the throat muscles taut but the mouth closed shut in typical Germanic stoicism. The eyes had clouded over, the light gone from them when the heart stopped.

Walker and Jack walked around the body without saying a word. In front of the dead man was an SS uniform, folded neatly in a stack. The shirt's right collar patch bore the runic double lightning bolts, the left patch and matching right shoulder board said, with its three diamonds and two double bars, Hauptsturmführer, Captain. His .32 was holstered and at his feet, next to his shined boots.

Jack had already processed the scene. "Ready?"

* * *

They descended the stairway towards the exit. Both stopped to look at the display of the hydrocephalic baby inside a formaldehyde jar. They each contemplated it for a few seconds and said nothing, because there was nothing to say.

"What do you think, Walker?" was the question once they were outside.

"The Inspector said our stiff was a medical man but there was no serpent badge on the uniform. That tells me he wasn't in the Medical Corps. He was standard SS, maybe with some medical knowledge, but no doctor, so I don't know why the Inspector would say he did medical experiments, unless that report he handed you says something different."

"Anything else?"

"Those slacks," Walker said. "They had cat hair on them."

"So the dead guy either had a cat—"

"Or the killer has one. And another thing: those clothes were pressed and regulation-folded. The killer knows how the Nazis folded their uniforms. Since those clothes were ironed and starched, our stiff wasn't wearing them when he was killed. Day or night, nobody would walk through Vienna wearing that uniform. The clothes either were placed in front of him as he was dying, or after he was dead. It's staged to make a statement. Question is, where did his street clothes go?"

Jack touched his breast pocket, where the Inspector's report rested. "We have another problem, Walker."

"And what might that be?"

Jack was quiet.

"What? You want me to chase down an orange cat?"

"Relax, Walker. The Inspector's report was in German, which is why I didn't show it to you."

"So my German isn't perfect, but I can manage. What does it say?"

"It gives us the man's name."

They stood outside together as the sun came up. Jack glanced upward to the stone turret from hell. "The man was on our list. Either way we'll never be able to talk to the Captain."

They walked to the curb together. Jack hailed a cab, opened up the suicide door, got in, but delayed the driver with a few words in German, and from the car window gave an order to Walker.

"There'll be a report on your desk in the morning. Read it then, and we'll talk"

He banged on the side door as a signal to the driver to take off.

Chapter Two

Every city breathes. Paris exhaled diesel fumes, fresh-pulled espresso and the strong perfume of either Gauloises or Gitanes cigarettes. Vienna, these days after the War, struggled for something between fresh air and ruin.

Life had to go onward and forward into tomorrow, and the day after. Not all the mornings were good, but there was coffee, and it was coffee at home or at the café that lured people out of bed, to splash water on their faces, dress and go to work. The beverage was less bitter than life in a new but damaged world. Each day began with a ritual, a return to simple things. There was the kiss of the match to a cigarette, and the promise of a breakfast pastry. People yearned for it, wanted it. Nobody had forgotten pleasures, such as butter and sugar because they were rationed during the war. Cupboards ran bare, cars sat idle without gasoline because civilization had come to a full stop. It was the slow return, in small increments of pleasure and luxury that put the word good before morning in Guten Morgen.

Walker took a deep breath and crossed the room to his office. The eyes at the desks followed him, as they had every day since his first week on the job. He felt queer in civilian clothes. He wore a navy suit, though he was an army man. His blue shirt met the military definition of crisp. His tie, black with diagonal red and blue stripes, gave him a businesslike appearance. His most comforting fashion accessory, Grable, hung secure inside a shoulder holster, a subtle lump under the suit jacket and invisible under the topcoat.

There was no nameplate on his door. The secretary Jack had assigned him was a young woman, devoid of personality and nondescript to the point of anonymity. Aside from the dress, there were no curves to her personality. She despised vices, particularly alcohol and tobacco. She seldom spoke, and her answers were always perfunctory and to the point. She was efficiency personified.

This morning, though, she did something different, something that almost showed character. Upon his arrival, when he threw his routine nod her way, she tilted her head to the door as her way of telling him something or someone was waiting for him inside. He braced himself and entered the room to find nothing but his desk and Jack's report.

He hung up his jacket and looked to his desk. Atop the brown folder was a white envelope addressed in a familiar hand. On the outer fold was written in black ink, "Your German word of the day is DER ZUGANG." Jack made it a habit of giving him pertinent vocabulary, in German, with the article so he would learn the gender, and with a brief definition.

On the surface, the word was an administrative term, meaning an entrance, but he knew that Jack had invited him to find a deeper definition, one related to the contents in the folder. Walker lowered himself into his leather chair. The billiard-green blotter on the desk rested on an oak battleground with writing instruments to the east and a telephone to the west.

He opened the folder flat on the desk so nobody could see its contents through the window behind him. He thought to draw the curtains, but sunlight was a luxury in Vienna. To the left was one page of typewritten notes in purple ink, the page held in place with a butterfly clasp. To the right was a stack of black and white photographs.

The first two revealed what a Mosin-Nagant rifle could do to a human head at several hundred yards. Walker read the notes and recognized the name of the dead man. The spitzer bullet had decapitated the target, and the impact tore the arms from the body upon impact. The man had been shot where the locals ate. Walker wondered what the scene did to the stomachs of the lunch crowd in the vicinity. His eyes crawled over the ballistics statement that indicated the distance and the angle from sniper's nest to kill.

Impressive.

A third picture was of a typical city square, a statue of a long-dead German elector centerstage. The fourth picture was of the recovered rifle, the sights made of iron and no fix to accept a bayonet. Atypical for the Russian sniper rifles he'd seen in the field. There was a bag next to the rifle. He perused the synopsis. No fingerprints. No other evidence. Not even a casual cigarette butt to let anyone know what brand the shooter preferred or how much time he had waited for his target.

More photographs, but these were of another crime scene.

A dead man lay fetal-like on a tiled bathroom-floor, surrounded by puddles of blood and excrement, his own pants down around his ankles, the face contorted in such agony that another photograph from more dignified times was necessary for identification.

According to the report, the victim had a fondness for custom-ordered sausage. The cause of death had not been poison, but rather the meat inside the casing had been laced with jaggedly cut bay leaves, which perforated the man's intestines during digestion. Local authorities interrogated every butcher in a ten-mile radius, thinking that a person or persons unknown had tampered with the meat. COD or Cause of Death, the medical examiner declared: 'Internal hemorrhaging related to perforations of the viscera.'

Walker rotated the drama in front of him. He imagined this ingenious but slow death, worthy of Dante's imagination. He realized from these photographs that forensic photography was a barbaric art form, a new pornography.

The last photograph was of a suspect: a man in his twenties, handsome in an ethnic sort of way. Walker looked to the left again and saw the words under the man's name: "Jew. Rape. Sonderkommando."

Walker read ethnicity, crime, and he parsed the foreign word.

Commando was a cognate, and the prefix 'Sonder' in German meant 'Special.' Walker concluded that Sonderkommando was the equivalent to the US Army's MOS, or Military Occupational Specialty.

The man's age bothered him, not that a man needed to be of age for violence. He had seen his share, done his share, a few short years ago. The phone rang.

Walker picked up the receiver and cradled it against his ear. "Yes."

"Review the folder?"

"Yes."

"Your opinion?"

"Inventive, intelligent, highly competent, and this is very, very personal."

Jack asked, "Familiar with chess?"

"I know what the pieces can do, but that's the extent of it. Why?"

"The German word I gave you, Der Zugzwang, is used in chess; it's what your opponent says when he wants you to make your move, but there's more to it than that."

"Why am I not surprised, Jack?"

"You say it when you have pressed your opponent into making a bad move."

"What do you want me to do?"

"Initiate contact with our young friend, and take a detail with you. He frequents a café over at Dorotheergasse. The place has excellent pastries. You can practice your German."

"And when I meet our friend?"

"Tell him that he needs to stop, but feel him out, determine his disposition."

"Understood, and disposition for what exactly?"

"See if you sense whether he could see our way of thinking or not."

Walker said, "Meaning we could use him."

"He's demonstrated creativity and commitment. Walker?"

"Yeah."

"Whittaker should pay him a visit after your talk with him."

Walker hung up the phone and stared at it for a moment. Jack Marshall was a Company man. They both went back to some ugly days in beautiful Italy, although it wasn't beautiful at the time. He was in Vienna at Jack's request. He figured that with no girl waiting for him back home, no family to speak of, it was the practical and prudent choice.

The rest of the office knew Jack as Mr. Marshall. Walker respected Jack because he possessed that personal touch for leadership. It had been demonstrated in combat and it made a clear transition to the office. Jack was decisive. Although he was no master of rhetoric, Jack could work a typewriter if he had to, or pick up the telephone to make an important call, or use a gun. He had executive abilities because he created solutions to complicated situations.

Walker closed the folder. He went to the window behind his desk. The view was of a half-dead Vienna, trying hard to come back to life. Stephanplatz had been bombed into despair during the War. Now everybody who was anybody was carving up the city and country.

He examined the Viennese sky. It was the dull kind of sky that you could never love unless you lived there all your life, the kind that reminded you that you were a foreigner.

Ein Ausländer.

Chapter Three

It was about half-past eight when Sheldon entered the café on his day off from work. He lived on the third floor above the establishment and over bookshop on the second floor. He found himself a quiet table, his back to the wall, with a clear view of the front door.

He ordered himself a grosser schwarzer and the café's pride, a warm buchtel filled with levkar jam topped with powdered sugar. He contemplated the plate and his coffee, with a devotion that bordered religious. A little girl with the widest eyes and blondest curls walked past him, one hand clutched in her father's and the other holding a wrapped, warm apfelstrudel. She smiled, and he smiled back.

He took one bite of his pastry, powdered sugar clinging playfully to his lips, when a man in a light overcoat, navy suit, blue shirt, and an unfortunate black tie with stripes pulled the chair across from him out with a metallic shudder that made the teeth itch. The face was shaven, features cast of solid bone, little feeling, and a trace of lethal innocence.

Sheldon looked up at his uninvited guest. "Do we know each other?"

"No. We should have a talk though."

"What about?" Sheldon sipped some of his strong coffee, which cleared his mind of any morning cobwebs. He wiped the sugar off his lips.

"I have seen your work. Quite impressive and creative."

"Thank you. I've been told as a tailor that I handle material well."

Sheldon took another sip. His eyes did not move from the man across from him.

"And I thought *coy* meant wearing a dress. I'm not talking about suits and slacks. Spare me the bit about being a tailor. That's your cover. I saw the rifle. The safety on it isn't worth a damn. Like I said, nice work. And my respect to you that you made the shot at that distance without a scope. Smart, too, because no scope means no glare, which means nobody knew you were there. How you didn't dislocate your shoulder when the rifle went off is another thing. That particular rifle is known to kick like a mule, and you're a tiny guy, but hey, looks are deceiving."

Sheldon studied the foreigner. There was a good brain behind the bad German.

His guest placed his elbows on the table for effect. "There's this little Finnish guy, about your height, who killed a couple hundred Germans. He used iron sights and even packed the snow in front of him so there was no puff of snow when the shot went off. There was nothing to give him away. Then one day a mortar shell wiped the smile off his little blonde face. He lived. I do not know if he smiles, but he lived. Get my point? You do have a nice smile. It would be a shame to see it changed permanently."

A waiter came up to the table.

"I'd like a coffee, please," the man said, badly mangling the umlauted verb.

"What variety would you like," the waiter asked in slow and polite German.

A blank stare overcame the American's face.

"He will have what I'm having," Sheldon said.

"Thank you," the guest said after the waiter walked off.

Sheldon spoke. "It's always appreciated when a foreigner tries in the language. Möchte, while legitimate, sounds too formal. He'll bring you the same order as mine—coffee, black and strong, and the same pastry. We can talk in English."

"Thanks. I appreciate it." And like that, the American's tough-guy persona disappeared. "As I was saying, I saw your work. You can play dumb all you want, but—"

"I have no idea what you're talking about. I was enjoying my breakfast on my day off when you showed up."

The coffee arrived with the pastry.

"I may not have figured you out, brother, but I'm not dumb. You seem too young for this line of work even if you say you're a tailor. Then again, I've seen kids fighting during the last days of the war, so maybe that rifle says you wore a Russian uniform."

"What rifle?"

"Don't play cute with me. Were you a sniper during the war?"

"No. I was too busy enjoying the hospitality the Nazis gave me in Birkenau."

The American's face dropped at the revelation.

"But you're Russian, right?"

"In a way, yes."

"I read the word 'Special Commando,' which could explain the skill with the rifle."

"You seem to know a lot about me."

"I know things, but 'why' is the biggest piece of the puzzle for me." He struck a match and lit his cigarette, waved the match out. "May I smoke?"

"If you must."

"Look, it isn't that we aren't sympathetic, but—"

"We? I see only you."

Sheldon looked to the window and saw two men, both in overcoats. Both men were hulks, and by the looks of them, not into the gentle art of crochet. The taller one, the one with the eyeglasses, looked like his hands could tear the spine out of a man for saying the wrong thing to his grandmother. His partner was the sensitive, intellectual type. He chewed his gum so rapidly his jaw pulsed faster than a cat's heartbeat.

"Stop what you're doing and you'll never meet them, but continue down this path then that is a different matter altogether."

Sheldon sipped and listened.

"Look, I'm just trying to help you. Back off, before you have a mishap like that Finnish fellow. The games in this town get kind of rough, I hear."

Sheldon sipped again.

"Every day in the newspaper there is some story about a guy who accidentally walked into a knife six or seven times, or hanged himself after kicking in his own ribs. You have no idea what you're walking into."

Sheldon responded. "Odd coming from a man who can't order a cup of coffee in decent German. You see that table over there on my left? That's where people put their newspapers for other customers to read after they're done. You'll find the newspapers there in any one of four languages, none of them English."

"LookI'm trying to be nice. I don't have culture; don't need it. I'm not paid to read Thomas Mann or contemplate all the delicacies of Proust's madeleine. Life is complicated. If you would like for me to draw you a little map, I will.

"Please do."

"Caesar has divided this country into four parts between the French, the Brits, the Russians, and yours truly, the ugly American. I don't know your argument with the dead Nazis, nor do I really care because dead is dead, but don't get any ideas about continuing your crusade here. This city may have been beautiful at one time, but right now it has some ugly growing pains to get through."

A quiet sip, a quick eye back to the overcoats outside. "I have no idea what you're talking about. I know nothing about dead Nazis. But since you're here in town, do I call you Wyatt Earp?"

"I'm partial to Doc Holliday myself."

Sheldon knew that the British were at the Schönbrunn Palace and the Hotel Sacher. The Russians took up residence in the Hotel Imperial and at the Palais Epstein. The French enjoyed the Kummer Hotel. The Americans placed themselves next to the money at the Oesterreichische Nationalbank but they could be found at the Hotel Bristol. Everyone in Vienna knew this the same way a desert nomad knows that a camel spits.

"For someone who likes Doc Holliday, you carry Caesar's eagle. Now that I've heard the imperial message and bought the messenger breakfast, it would be nice if I had a name to go with the face. That way we won't be strangers should there be a next time."

The request for his name made him squint. "Walker. My name is Walker."

"That a first name or last?"

"Does it matter? And since we are all nice and cozy and acquainted, what's yours?"

"Sheldon, but something tells me you knew that."

Walker rose, all six-foot-two of him and picked up his hat with his first two fingers. He played with the two dimples of the fedora, ran his thumb along the brim. For a second it seemed as if he was going to say something, but in the end, he decided to keep it simple. "Thanks for breakfast."

When the American moved a short distance from the table, Sheldon called out, "Walker?"

Walker turned to the voice.

"That tie. You need to do something about that tie."

Walker's left hand ironed the tie against his chest. "What's wrong with it?"

"You could do better. Remember, I'm a tailor."

Chapter Four

Walker was tired. He was new to the job, better than raw meat, but a fresh recruit nonetheless. There was the language, the first tastes of success at communication followed by failures. People spoke slang. People spoke fast and they used colloquial phrases and verbs not in any of his grammar books. There was so much information that his nerves went out of tune like a piano after a student of Beethoven pounded the keys.

The dim light from behind the curtains comforted him. He fell back onto the bed. His body sighed into the mattress. He didn't dream of knights, damsels in distress, or of some heroic quest. Instead, his mind reeled in bright sun, clean air, the smell of laundry and the face of his mother in the kitchen. She was doing the dishes. Coffee sang strong in the air. He watched her, child-like. His hand tugged at her skirt and she smiled at him.

The image of her faded to white. He realized he was outside, visiting his aunt. The field of corn ran out to a horizon of blue sky in Middle America. He and his aunt were leaving services, the shake of the Reverend's firm grip fresh in his hand. He walked down the steps of the church in his proud suit. He had looked up at the steeple, the cloudless sky. He saw his aunt saying something to him about lunch as they walked past the picket-fence cemetery, where the slats of wood kept the dead quarantined from the living world.

His body moved a little. His head turned, and in his mind was Peggy with her ponytail and hay in her hair. She had coaxed him into the barn and taught him love before he associated it with the smell of perfume, stale cigarettes, and regret. He looked up at her, felt her warm hand on the side of his face and her hot skin against his. It was the only time he thought sweat smelled innocent. She rested with him in the loft of the red barn in the middle of a different world.

His eyelids twitch and now he was finishing boot camp. He received medic training. He remembers the day he first wore his dress uniform. He had received his commission. He remembers Henry. They shared cigarettes. They pooled their change to buy beer. They flirted with girls and laughed off their romances. He met other girls, but always thought of Peggy and the sweeping movement of her hair caught up in the ponytail.

Then came the bitter cold, horrible noises, the confusion that day behind the patch of dirt nobody would call a hill. The bullets came in like angry bugs that died in the dirt. There was so much chaos the ears hummed and the eyes had to see and hear the hell around him. Henry was there, scared like him. He went to say something to Henry, when a bullet went through his friend's cheek and stole the smile and half of his face.

Walker's feet sliced the open air at the edge of the mattress. He was moving through trees like matchsticks, as he searched for Jack. There was gunfire, the scent of gunpowder in the wintry air, his heartbeat in his throat. He found Jack wounded and attended to him. He heard Jack say something and instinctively spun with Grable, shooting Germans, before he took a bayonet from a Fritz, who was dying much younger, more handsome than Walker was in that small patch of snow in the forest.

He woke up and gasped for air.

* * *

Walker returned to the office. Miss Nobody at the desk reminded him that he had an appointment. Walker knew what it meant and with whom. Walker kept his topcoat on and began the path to the door.

Jack Marshall worked in a new office with an old view. The air inside was always keen although Walker never could quite locate the source for the cold temperature. The air moved with an undetectable chill. The five-sided room came to a point behind the desk where two windows displayed two distinct views of the city that Germans called Wien. The left window revealed a decimated edifice that groaned its way up into the sky while the right window exhibited a modern striptease of decadence from the top down since Allied artillery had wiped away the top half of the building. The wood of his desk would turn amber under the sunlight through these two windows.

Jack was a thoroughbred of a man with long legs and strode across rooms with ample grace. Jack hailed from Montana with violence in his blood from hunting and herding cattle. His eyes reminded you that he'd seen evil spirits. He wore burgundy brogues, and an olive suit out of loyalty to the US Army, and an open-collar white shirt with so much starch that Walker swore that if Jack tossed it to the ground the damn thing could stand at attention on its own. Like the way he enjoyed his whiskey straight, Jack was all business.

"You've met with the subject at the café?"

"I did."

Everything was important to Jack, but this particular case had floated to the top of his priorities after the file from Karlsruhe, a city in southwestern Germany and temporary HQ for the Company. Walker recounted every detail of the meeting to Jack, including his missteps.

"You need to work on your German," Jack said, in the way an older brother teased his younger one about homework or a girl. Walker accepted it because of their bond.

They had amassed an impressive series of combat decorations in the time it took them from the freezing hell of San Pietro, crossing of the Rapido River, the trek across the Meurthe River into the Colmar Pocket on the Alsatian Plains, and before they advanced onward through blood, snow, and more blood, they arrived at a concentration camp. The only two times Walker had seen Jack's veneer crack was when his dog had died and Dachau.

"About the word sonderkommando, sorry the dossier was incomplete, Walker."

"No worries here."

"Your initial instinct was right. It is very, very personal for our new friend."

"Think we can keep him on a leash?" Walker asked.

"Our conflict with him is when his list agrees with ours, which is the case with our dead Hans in the looney bin, but Karlsruhe has agreed to give him a pass."

"You disagree?" Walker asked.

"Hard not to sympathize, but I'm okay with clemency."

"What's the link between him and the photos in the file you left me?"

Walker wasn't mad that Jack hadn't clued him in on all the details. The notes Walker read were about as telegraphic and spotty as a convict's chance of steady employment.

Jack pulled open a desk drawer. He extracted two short glasses. Next, a bottle appeared. It was a man's medicine, renewable without a prescription. Jack poured out two neat slugs without the splash. He tossed the firewater back. Walker repeated the act and tightened his eyes for the heated fury in his throat.

Sunlight shone on Jack's chest and made the starched white shirt stark. "It is the damnedest thing, isn't it, Walker? Less than four years ago, the only good Gerry was a dead one, and now we're trying to keep some of them alive, sort them out for what they know about the Russians. We would've decorated Sheldon for killing Nazis, if he'd worn our uniform. Fruit salad on the chest and a slap on the back."

"Something tells me his body count is higher than we think."

Jack's hand mindlessly turned the label on the bottle to face him. The whiskey was twenty years old, smooth as if the Devil himself had made it. "You asked about a common link."

"I did, yes. Have something?"

"Karlsruhe says that those two stiffs you saw in the dossier worked at Auschwitz. As for body count, it looks like our friend at the café is good for eighteen kills."

"Fill in some holes for me, Jack. Like the word Sonderkommando, for example."

"They were special units, usually Jews. They were given better quarters, better food, and lived on borrowed time. We don't know how they were selected. Leslie will give us more details on asylum boy at another meeting."

Jack retrieved a photograph from a folder near him. He pushed it toward

Walker.

"The headless corpse was an SS guard. He ran the prisoner barracks." Jack's forefinger tapped the corner of the photograph, "He did smuggling on the side, had his way with some of the Polish girls, and then after the war became a small-town politician. Nobody second-guessed his past. He sailed through denazification and continued his smuggling operation."

Walker asked, "What did he move?"

"Anything that made money, but he was partial to art and rare treasures. He was part of Göring's masterplan to make Linz the art center of Nazi Europe. The Venus fixers have started a file on the creep."

"And the operators in his network—active or disbanded after the war?"

"Don't know, but we might have a diagram on the blackboard in about twenty years."

Walker rolled a Camel in the front of his lips, teasing out a loose thread of tobacco before he lit the cigarette. "Why the payback?"

"This picture might explain it." Jack's finger flicked another photo, a new one, towards Walker. This one showed two men with five-cent minds in fifty-dollar suits with the deceased some time before his head came off his shoulders.

"So Sheldon waited for him a half-mile away with a rifle in a nest?" Walker was again impressed with the fatal shot. The rifle used without a scope was supposedly accurate to 400 meters.

"The shot would've made a Marine proud." Jack re-examined the photograph and Walker saw the look of admiration in his friend's face. "And that brings us to our next victim, the man on the toilet. A real mess, don't you think?"

"Sight and smell must've been a pucker moment."

"It turns out this gentleman had an unhealthy interest in young boys before, during, and after the War, which gives the method to his demise a perverse yet poetic irony."

Walker said, "Butchers were interviewed, and it came to nothing."

Jack waved the photo. "The bay leaves worked like razor blades through his system."

"When I saw the word "Rape" in the file I had assumed it meant Sheldon was a rapist, and that he was Russian prisoner of war."

Jack shook his head. "Sheldon was the one raped, in Auschwitz, and we're gray by whom. Few survivors of the camps discuss the horrors they've experienced, but we do know the survivors don't look kindly upon Sonderkommandos. I can't imagine it."

"Imagine what?" Walker asked.

"To be, thrown into a hell-hole like Auschwitz, thought of as a traitor, and handle the dead the way the Sonderkommandos were asked to as they themselves were purged every now and then, and then get raped."

A cloud covered the sun. The room turned crimson.

"I empathize with Sheldon," Walker said.

"It's tempting, but don't. Sheldon can have any Nazis who are useless to us. If we can't use them or blackmail them, Sheldon can take them. I have no qualms about that, since we know more than a few escaped the hangman's noose, but he can't run wild."

Walker had to ask, "And if he isn't content with scraps?"

Jack sighed. "We take the necessary measures."

"Put a line through his name?"

"At the moment, he knows we exist and he knows we know. It's wait and see."

Walker looked out the leftmost window and saw the edifice. He never liked marble. The stone could last forever but as it aged, it faded to dust and the scent suggested decay.

Chapter Five

Walker's words troubled Sheldon enough that he replayed each and every sentence in English and German in his mind. Even days after, when he saw the Prater's Riesenrad, the giant Ferris wheel, he couldn't help but think that the wheel of Fate had broken a spoke and come tumbling down after him.

Sheldon left his flat above the bookshop in the sixth district for a trip outside the city. On his way out, he passed by the maintenance man's workroom. The door was closed, but behind it Sheldon heard a sad and wounded sound. He didn't know what to make of it. He'd seen the door open once. Inside the room was a bench with many tools on the wall, and scattered about the space numerous mops, buckets, and the usual disinfectants and cleansing agents. And now, this forlorn and awful noise.

He was intrigued but shook it off. He needed to clear his own head and search the sky, somewhere outside of Vienna, where he could see trees and rocks. He checked that he had his identification papers in his pocket. He had packed a few slices of hard bread, some fig jam, and a small amount of cheese into a small basket along with a sturdy wine glass. He figured that he could purchase wine from one of the many family shops on his way.

Aboard the tram he sat observant as the transport moved toward the end of the line. Trains haunted him, but this one had open windows and the overhead wires sizzled. This street car didn't have many passengers, dying or dead, and the view was of a numb city instead of an endless flatland, deaf trees, and the gate of hell for a destination.

Inside the compartment's square space, there were some hungry eyes and hard faces, and somebody's dog was on the floor who was seeing legs as a forest or as a world of wonder. A woman opposite him fished out a tube of cream and applied it, first on her fingernails, rubbing the moisture in, then, squeezed some more onto her knuckles.

Across from Sheldon sat a Madonna and child tightly huddled, two scared Hungarians. The mother wore a dirty bonnet and kept touching her daughter's clothes and hair, either to smooth out her own anxiety or remove the dirt of the world with each stroke.

At the end of the line he left the tram and began the trek. He repeated his conversation with Walker in his mind again and again, as his feet chewed their way up the tight switchbacks to summit Kahlenberg, where the open air, the view, put his heart through his knees and into the ground. From a small constellation of trees he looked towards heaven, seeing Vienna in the distance, and realized then and there it had become a city of hard decisions and few choices.

Chapter Six

The city air came up in the morning, like it always does, cold, damp, and forgetting yesterday.

Since Jack discerned no immediate connection between Sheldon to the dead man in the tower, his instructions to Whittaker were to question Sheldon zealously, and the adverb *zealously,* was worrisome since Whittaker was a man who was literal.

Whittaker was a cinderblock of a man from the Lower East Side with a look that had served him well in infiltrating the criminal underworld of Vienna. When he spoke like a Yid or played the Dago or some other working-class miserable, crooks, felons, and thugs believed him. But back in their army days he was a different man, the jester with a pair of dice in his back pocket. In combat, Whittaker was the man who could convince soldiers that pulling a grenade pin with your teeth was possible.

Whittaker was promoted fast, which would've surprised people in the military had they known he was Puerto Rican on his mother's side. His father's Anglo name had fooled people. He was 'Top Kick,' a First Sergeant, a taskmaster, strict but fair and not without a sense of humor.

There was that time when he had caught privates and corporals smoking in a non-designated area. The men thought he'd cut them some slack because he walked past them. Whittaker waited until a half hour before reveille and woke up the company by clanging a large ladle against a metal garbage can. After the men mustered outside, he had them collect cigarette butts and deposit them into a large pail. Whittaker informed them the cigs they had retrieved represented their dead comrades. He distributed shovels and ordered them to dig a grave, six feet by six feet. The men broke earth and buried all their friends.

When they completed the task, Top Kick appeared, reviewed the work, and instructed them that, unfortunately, orders had come down and the grave had to be moved. The men dug up their dead and re-interred them at another location, where Whittaker then gave a eulogy.

Whittaker was the man who got things done, although you didn't want to know how it was done. And now he'd said that Sheldon would 'be gotten.'

Walker on the edge of his bed, stared at his nightstand, at Grable. He was uncertain about the job, about Vienna, and whether Jack's dispatching Whittaker after Sheldon was the right thing to do without more evidence.

There was no evidence that Sheldon was the killer. There were no witnesses. Nothing.

Walker sympathized with Sheldon, now that Jack filled in details not in the file. The Nazis had started the mess. They were the ones who had stuck whole nations into ovens. They were the ones who had followed a little runt Catholic who couldn't grow a moustache right, let alone comb his hair. Walker thought about the dead SS Captain at the Fruitcake House, clothes at his feet. Why didn't the uniform match his MOS, his military occupational specialty? After wearing out the floorboards, Walker returned and sat down on the edge of the bed.

He picked up Grable. He took her apart, cleaned her, and reassembled her in a calm, methodical manner. It was hygiene, the field strip procedure. He could take Grable down to her pins and springs in under thirty seconds, and reassemble her in a minute. It comforted him to take apart and put back together the very thing that had saved his life multiple times.

He took deep calming breaths. He had repeated this same meditative exercise with Grable in Italy, France, and finally, Germany. Countless times. He remembered the peace with which he did this procedure, in all types of weather. The few seconds of love assured him that he would have more hours of life.

He put on his jacket. He checked his reflection in the bathroom mirror and concluded Sheldon was right. The tie had to go.

* * *

At a corner shop Walker practiced his German, obtained his cup of joe from the vendor, and paid for his drink before he walked to the office. He had delayed the inevitable. He needed to see Leslie.

Leslie came to them through Major General Davies, Jack' superior in Karlsruhe, who was convinced that her talents would help the Company. Jack confessed to Davies that he wasn't thrilled about the prospect of another woman in the office. Women were good as secretaries, Jack said, but Davies insisted that Leslie was an invaluable asset because, as the General phrased it, 'she has a masculine mind for details, above-average intelligence with operations, and field experience.' It was the last part of Davies's assessment, however, that took hold of Jack's eyebrows: 'She is the deadliest shot I've seen, male or female, in my career.'

Fluent in German, Czech, French, and passable in Russian, Leslie was the author of effective propaganda used in pamphlet-drops to get disaffected German civilians and military personnel to flip to the Allied cause.

Her field experience was equally impressive. Hours before a high-ranking SS officer was scheduled to interrogate a Resistance member at a secluded and secured location, she arrived, disguised as a secretary. She had so convinced the guards that she was authorized to record the prisoner's preliminary testimony that they let her into the compound. When the SS officer arrived, he found two dead guards and an empty room.

Leslie's most remarkable feat, according to Davies, was her chumming up a mark, an SS colonel, known to like redheads and privy to Himmler's darkest desires. Leslie metamorphosed herself into a lethal Rita Hayworth. With her long legs in a tight dress and in high heels that added a tilt to her gait, she stripped the colonel of sensitive information over several weeks of pillow talk and cigarettes. The intelligence that she had extracted in the boudoir proved devastating to the Nazis. Hitler had the officer tortured, strung up with piano wire, until he confessed to his failure to the Fatherland.

Jack gave her an office of her own, which prompted rumors.

Leslie arrived in Vienna with a different look altogether. She sported a

Louise Brooks bob and an archaic cloche that she wore intentionally to make others think she was older than she was and to offset any suspicion of an unaccompanied woman in a car traveling into Vienna. The War was over but a Nazi bounty persisted over her heart-shaped face.

Chapter Seven

Walker walked into a room full of whispers, typewriters clacking, their bells strong and loud on carriage returns, and air that smelled of coffee, cigarettes, and the occasional whiff of perfume.

He had accepted that whatever it was that had happened between Whittaker and Sheldon was done and in the past, although there were no details, no report from Whittaker, or any updates. None of it mattered since Whittaker was not an office man. He preferred the field. He kept to himself, abhorred the written word and had no use for phones.

A secretary's cough stopped Walker. Her eyes told him where he was to go next. He folded his coat over his arm, made certain that his blazer was buttoned, and walked to Jack's office, realizing that he had been seeing more of Jack's office than his own of late.

He knocked and after he heard Jack call him in from the other side of the door, he pushed it open, hung his topcoat up, and waited for Jack to finish his phone call. Walker saw Leslie in the room and said hello. Jack's hand indicated a chair. Jack's mouth said all the polite and managerial things before he placed the receiver back into the cradle.

"The amount of incompetence in our government astounds me. That was a fellow from the SSU in Karlsruhe. He insists we set up shop in Munich. I imagine there will be staff meetings to decide on the wallpaper."

The SSU was the Strategic Service Unit. In Jack's eyes, the one vowel was not enough to distance the SSU from its predecessor, OSS, the Office of Strategic Services. He admired Wild Bill Donovan and one of Donovan's undercover agents, Lieutenant John Hamilton. He had less admiration for their successors.

"This fellow told me a civilian from some oversight committee will deliver a list of names for us to investigate. Leslie, you'll be happy to know that Major General Davies is accompanying this civilian. This list of his is the result from the latest interrogations. I don't like sloppy seconds from SSU, but protocol is protocol. Walker, I'd like you to review the list."

Walker acknowledged the assignment.

Jack turned his attention to Leslie. "What do we have on the recent find at the asylum?"

Leslie parted a folder, took out two pages. "Hope both of you skipped breakfast."

Jack and Walker had seen too many things to feel queasy.

"The physician at the scene said carbolic acid, right?" she asked.

Walker remembered the verdict in German. Abgespritzt.

"He did," Jack said. "Injected in the arm instead of the heart. Is that significant?"

"Carbolic acid, also known as phenol, was used at Auschwitz as a killing method for the sick and unproductive workers. The main camp kept the chemical in its pharmacy under the pretense it would be used for eardrops." Leslie consulted the second page. "I researched what I could of the Nuremberg Medical Trial transcripts for other drugs. Since the trial of Nazi doctors ended last year, not everything is available to me, but I managed to dig up more information on the man."

Jack sensed something when she hesitated. "Is something wrong?"

"Mengele used phenol, but the name most associated with the chemical was a Dr. Friedrich Entress. Executed last year. He was an enthusiastic little sadist, even by Nazi standards. Entress started out with TB and typhus patients, but then he delegated injections, which brings us to our friend in the asylum."

She handed Jack the second piece of paper. Jack pronounced the name in perfect German and translated some biographical facts for Walker. "Anything else?" Jack asked.

"Other than he carried out injections for Entress, he also had a hand in clinical trials."

"What clinical trials?" Jack asked.

"More experiments?" Walker asked.

"Yes. Entress and other doctors received commissions for their research."

"Payments from whom?" Jack asked as he put the page down on his desk with disgust. Twenty of the 23 defendants were medical doctors, and the seven who were hanged were SS.

"IG Farben and Bayer. They paid the Nazi doctors to test their new inventions in the lab."

"Follow the money," Jack said.

The Farben trial would see 24 executives for defendants, 13 found guilty, the rest acquitted, and none executed. Businessmen were tried in the Flick and Krupp trials, and the results were either acquittals or modest prison sentences for crimes against humanity.

Walker's eyes blinked. "Our dead man was Igor to a Dr. Frankenstein?"

Jack interrupted. "Doesn't that seem unusual? To have someone with a rank doing the works of an orderly. Is it possible that a prisoner could've been involved?"

"You think Sheldon decided to give the man a dose of his own medicine?" Walker asked.

Jack shrugged. "Why not?"

"I'm not convinced," Leslie answered. "If Sheldon knew about the medical experiments, I would think that he wouldn't have lived as long as he had in the camp. The more he escorted TB or typhus prisoners to their lethal injections, the greater his chances were of contracting those diseases, and let us not forget, the SS eliminated witnesses to what they were doing."

"So you don't think he did it?" Jack asked.

"I didn't say that. There's not enough evidence to tell."

"That reminds me," Jack said. "Either of you hear from Whittaker?"

Walker looked to Leslie and then answered, "Not a chirp."

Jack tapped his pencil like a baton, up and down to some unknown score. "That's odd not to hear a peep from him, but God knows the man stood a little too close to the artillery." He touched his temple with the pencil. "But he's a good egg."

There was a knock at the door.

It was one of the secretaries. When she had opened the door, her nails, done in a nice Japanese red maple, curled around the doorframe. "Excuse me, Mr. Marshall, but there is a man who wishes to see you."

"Who is it?" Jack asked.

Walker noticed that the office behind her was quiet.

There were no cicada-like conversations, no clickity-clack of typewriter keys, and no end-return carriage bells. Nothing. Jack and Leslie had noticed it, too.

The secretary blushed a shade close to the one on her fingernails. "He says his name is Sheldon."

"Show him in." If Jack was surprised, his officer training deflected it.

Sheldon strode into the office, his hat in his left hand. He wore a tailored brown suit, a white shirt with thin pinstripes. It was a dapper custom look if you ignored the bruise on his left cheek.

"That'll be all, Leslie," Jack said.

She gathered her things, looking both annoyed and concerned and walked past Sheldon.

"Thank you for seeing me, gentlemen," Sheldon said in neutral English. If he had an accent, Walker's ears weren't sharp enough to identify it. "I've met Walker over breakfast, but I don't think we've had the pleasure. I believe you are Mr. Marshall."

"I am." Jack rose. "Please come in."

Walker offered Sheldon his chair. Sheldon thanked him. Walker pretended to look at something outside the window but he listened to everything behind him.

"I hope that I am not too much of an interruption, Mr. Marshall."

"No trouble at all. What can I do for you?"

"It seems that someone felt it necessary to send me a message. I had the pleasure of meeting a very enthusiastic man, although he didn't seem the type of man I'd associate with this office. Whittaker was his name and a colleague of yours."

Jack asked, "And how is Whittaker?"

Sheldon shrugged. "I haven't the slightest idea, Mr. Marshall."

Jack absorbed the response without emotion. "I see. As for that message, we were concerned that our business and your personal plans might get mixed up. I thought Whittaker could provide some clarification, but ..." There was a small pause, one that Walker associated with Jack and danger, "since he isn't here and you are, perhaps we can discuss matters."

Sheldon grinned as he looked Jack in the eyes. Walker couldn't decide which unnerved him more, the smile or Sheldon's stare. "Might I ask what kind of business is done here?"

Jack didn't hesitate. "We are an assurance company."

"I see." Sheldon's voice had taken a dry tone.

"And what kind of business are you in?"

"I'm a tailor, Mr. Marshall. I'm sure Walker said as much after our breakfast together."

"Ah, yes. You're a tailor."

Walker glanced at Sheldon's hand, certain Jack had noticed it earlier. Sheldon placed both hands on the armrests. The knuckles were chafed and purple as an eggplant.

Jack said, "About that conversation with Whittaker. The two of you talk long?"

"He left in a hurry. I don't know why since I was very polite to him. I answered all his questions. Maybe he needed to think my answers through. My impression of Whittaker is that he is not what one would call a deep thinker. He was abrupt and left. There does seem to be a lack of manners in the world today."

"I'll see to it that Whittaker receives a refresher on social skills." Jack's voice had teeth. "Might I ask, what are your plans in Vienna?"

The sunlight had faded inside the office and Walker saw Sheldon's eyes change from light blue to a dark ocean. "An assurance company like yours must have access to my official file. As for plans, I hope to set up a permanent shop in Vienna."

Jack remained composed and emotionless. "We do have access to your papers. I learned you were a sonderkommando, which some might say is as good as being a collaborator. I ask because, unlike most Jews, your papers don't indicate an interest in moving to Palestine."

Walker saw no reaction to Jack's bait.

"It seems your file on me is incomplete and inaccurate."

Jack's face twitched.

Sheldon placed his hat on Jack's desk. Jack looked at it. He blinked and refocused his eyes on the man in front of him. Sheldon pulled forward the sleeves of his shirt so that they peeked out from under his suit-jacket. "As we say in my profession, let's tidy up some loose threads, shall we?"

Jack didn't move and neither did Walker. "I am a tailor," Sheldon said. "You know where I work. Walker and then Whittaker found me easy enough. As for being a Jew and a camp survivor, I am afraid you are half-correct. Technically, I'm Russian, and if you bothered to look into the matter of my time in the Lager you will find that as a Kommando I disposed of the dead. We did none of the killing. I was not a collaborator. It's not anger or bitterness you hear in my voice, Mr. Marshall, it's disappointment that Americans fail to look beneath the surface of matters." Sheldon's pause was intended to lure Jack into the net.

Jack said, "Disappointment?"

"After the hostilities ended, I gave detailed testimony and identified many of the war criminals at Auschwitz and others who had passed through the camps. Nazis. Industrialists of various nationalities, including Americans. I provided names and descriptions, but it seemed it was not in your country's interest to make all of them accountable. But, I understand why."

"Why is that?" Jack asked.

"Money. Politics."

"And Palestine?"

"I survived one hell, Mr. Marshall, so why would I want to walk into another one? You are aware of the fierce quarrels within Jewish groups and with the British over Palestine here in Vienna? Why would I put myself anywhere near the Haganah, the Irgun, or the Lehi? Are you quick to forget the King David Hotel bombing?"

Sheldon paused. Walker's mind scrambled to find a foothold in the conversation. He could hear Jack take in air through his nostrils. It was an old army trick. A deep inhalation calmed the nervous system. Jack placed both his hands on the desk, one on top of the other.

"The British control the flow of Jews into Palestine," he said, "and you are correct; it is a mess. Jewish refugee factions, in and out of the Kaserne, are run by the Stern Gang and the Irgun. The problem is nobody knows what brand of Zionism will win out at the end of the day, so the Brits label groups of Jews over one hundred in number as requiring surveillance or, at the worst, say they are terrorists. As for the King David Hotel, people are curious to what degree the Russians supported the terrorist attacks against the British."

"The Nazis said the same thing about the Communists after the Reichstag fire, and along came Herr Hitler," Sheldon said. "But you've forgotten one thing."

"Have I?"

"You said nobody knows what version of Zionism will win the day. My question is this—nobody knows on which side of the Palestinian question the Americans will fall. Might I offer you an observation, Mr. Marshall?"

"Please do."

Sheldon crossed a leg. "My advice is derived from my experience in Auschwitz. To perceive the Russians accurately, you need to understand two things about them. The first is that Mother Russia cares only about her children. That means everybody who is not Russian is subject to review, including all of Central Europe. All the ethnic types, those other Slavs, they will do the dying first."

"A rather peculiar view since Stalin himself is not a Russian."

Sheldon smiled. "Very true, Mr. Marshall. But the man is in power, which brings me to the second thing you must know about Russia." He leaned forward in his chair. "This is the first time in her history that she has the boot on her foot and not on her neck. Anyone who has seen the Russians fight knows they have no fear of death."

Jack nodded. "I have seen the Russians fight, and as a military man I admire them. Times, however, have changed and there is a new situation in the world."

Sheldon picked up his hat, "No, Mr. Marshall, times have not changed. The camps are still full, except now they have Germans in them. And when the time comes, some of those who are in those camps will be sent to eastern Siberia. There is one last item, something I told your colleague Whittaker. It's something Americans seem to forget about the Russians."

"And what is that?" Jack asked.

"It's a good thing that Stalin is a cold-hearted man. If it were a different man in the chair Russia might not have been able to defeat Hitler. What you Americans need to understand is that the apparatchiks within the Cheka who hate the man believe in a new social reality as passionately as you do your *Stars and Stripes*. I said it to Whittaker and I'll repeat it you. You best reevaluate what you are walking into."

"I understand, Sheldon."

"Do you?"

"I do."

"Maybe the bigger picture here is everyone should clean their own house," Sheldon said, "especially the British. And maybe for you, here in this assurance company, the matter is to look around you. Many of our answers in life are often found closest to us, not outside. Oh and one more thing: I had nothing to do with the dead man in the Narrenturm."

Sheldon said good-bye and left.

Jack picked up his pencil and Walker heard, "Find Whittaker."

Chapter Eight

The next day, Walker rang Whittaker. No answer.

Whittaker's flat was in the British zone, over at Maxingstrasse, a pleasant out-of-the-way street between the Tiergarten and the Botanischer Garten, the zoo and garden, which were both popular with children.

Vienna was a big place for small kids after the War for all the wrong reasons. Walker saw children run feral in the bombed-out Favoriten, the working-class district. He watched mothers bring their kids, City Council coupons in hand, down to the Swedish Red Cross for shoes because there was a leather shortage. Children would run through the streets shoeless. And then there were the juvenile prisons for diminutive robbers and nymphet prostitutes.

Young girls sat in small private rooms, cells, really. The amenities included no roommate; one door, locked after hours; one bed, one toilet; one window for fresh air; one desk, and one uncomfortable chair that would make a hardened convict in America cry. Many of these girls received medical care for more than one venereal disease.

Walker smoked one of his Camels for breakfast.

At the charity houses, where school children sought food, visiting doctors classified children into three cohorts. 1 meant healthy, 2 meant not so healthy, and 3 meant six kilos underweight. Most of the children were 3s.

Both Walker and Jack had a soft spot for kids.

Jack would visit Bellevue Hospital in his off time. He donated money, discretely, in unchanged American bills in small denominations, to several relief organizations. Jack was particularly long in the face the day he came back to the office after he had seen an entire room of beds with children in stiff body jackets for spinal tuberculosis.

Over at St. Anna Kinderspitals, the preeminent pediatric hospital in Europe for childhood blood disorders and cancers, Walker befriended a child who fought off fevers, held strong against the disease that wasted away his body, yet the kid smiled whenever someone wanted to play a game. This kid loved having stories read to him, and Walker did that, in his imperfect German.

He went one day with a new book and found an empty bed.

Walker called Whittaker again. No answer.

Walker enjoyed a real breakfast near the animal houses at the Tiergarten. He ate a pastry in the spot Jean-Nicholas Jadot had designed. He enjoyed the frescoes from Ovid and wished he could recall the Latin of his schooldays. A sign said that the petting zoo was experiencing a delayed opening. Passing the Palmenhaus, Walker debated whether he wanted to see the greenhouse or visit a smaller greenhouse, or whether he wanted to see the butterflies and moths at the Schmetterlinghaus.

He used up the last of his change for another call. No answer.

Walker didn't last long in the butterfly house. He wiped the sweat off his forehead and the back of his neck with his handkerchief. Twice. He fanned his jacket with the illusion that a whisper of air might undo the stickiness between his shirt and skin.

He walked until he reached Whittaker's place. The building, with that Tyrolean look of dark wood timber against a whitewash wall, was wedged between a convenience kiosk and a private residence. He walked into the establishment.

"Guten Tag," Walker said to the man behind the counter.

The man waived away the German. "What can I do for you, American?"

"That obvious to you?"

The man shrugged. "You all look the same to me."

"I'm looking for a friend of mine. Room 305. Might you know if he is —"

"He not home."

Walker knew the man was telling the truth since Whittaker hadn't answered his phone.

"May I go up to the room and see if he is in?"

Walker decided that this exchange needed a little background music, so his hand went into his pocket. He pulled out Andrew Jackson. He figured Old Hickory was more persuasive and taller than Hamilton. The man snatched the bill off the counter.

After the shaky ride in the paternoster, Walker stepped off onto the landing of the third floor and looked back at the elevator. Vienna had more of these relics in use than he had thought. His list of things to dislike grew longer.

He studied the cheap brass numbers, 305, on the brown wood. The doorknob appeared to be grafted onto the door from some cheap yard-sale table. As he rapped on the old timber, the door creaked open and Walker felt a cool breeze.

He pulled Grable from her holster and his handkerchief from his breast pocket, using the hanky to push the door wide. His eyes searched the room for potential blind spots. There was nothing but silence, a curtain billowing from the breeze through an open window.

Whittaker was never a homemaker but he kept his room respectable as a barrack. His place would not have passed inspection with the drill instructor. The sheets were torn from the bed, and not from romance. Bureau drawers were pulled out, emptied upside down onto the floor. Clothes were underfoot as Walker canvassed the scene with Grable in one hand, handkerchief in the other. Nothing. He holstered her and, using the cloth on the knob, closed the door. Time for privacy, time to assess and reconstruct or deconstruct the mayhem.

There were no signs of human violence. No blood. Lamps were plugged in, so no sign of assault or garroting with the electrical cord. Mirrors intact. Hotel stationery present on the modest desk, but no messages, there or around the phone. Walker began to think of places Whittaker would have hidden anything.

He went into the bathroom. Everything was too bright, too white. Walker looked at the toilet with its white rim, white cover, white ascending pipe into the elevated cistern, also white, and the nickel chain hanging off the lever. Walker put down the seat. He had grown up with women so it was an old habit that most men never learned. Walker would joke that men would be more successful with women if they learned the simple act of putting the lid down.

He stepped onto the flat toilet lid. On his toes, he peeled the cistern lid off overhead and felt under the cool surface. He groped around. He skimmed the top of the water with his fingertips. He felt something odd. It escaped him at first but he pushed it to the side and dragged it up the side of the tank.

The square item was a floatable luggage tag, similar to a military ID tag. Inside it was a small, odd-shaped key to a safe-deposit box, a storage locker at a train station, a bus station, or some other place. He restored the lid to the cistern and stepped down from his perch and used his handkerchief to wipe away any trace of a footprint on the toilet lid.

Walker washed his hands, and the luggage tag, which he put into his coat pocket. He returned to the main room.

Something didn't feel right. He was missing something. He looked at the floor. No floorboards appeared loose. There was no artwork in the room. He reviewed the lamps again, and suddenly wondered why there were two. The one by the bed made sense, but the one at the desk didn't. The desk was in perfect position for sunlight and it looked like the street lamplight provided enough illumination for a quick nocturnal scribble. He picked up one of the hotel pads by its edges and examined it for pressure indentations. No indication of any writing. No surprise there. Whittaker was no intellectual.

The second lamp bothered him. He unplugged it and tested the spindle shaft, wiggled it, and appreciated its heft. He examined the lamp's base, unscrewed it. He looked down the dark tunnel and gave it a gentle shake, and out came a roll of cash wrapped around a small piece of steno paper with writing on it, and a red rubber band. Walker let the money fall on the desk before he pocketed it.

He screwed the lamp's base back into place and returned it to its original location. He retraced all his steps and erased all of his hand placements with the handkerchief before using it on the doorknob upon exiting.

The man downstairs wasn't going to like what housekeeping had to say later in the morning, but Walker figured the man could take up his complaint with Andrew Jackson.

On his way back through the zoo, Walker tossed his tie into a trash can.

Chapter Nine

There is Maxfield Parrish blue, Mediterranean blue, Prussian blue, and a variety of other shades for infinite seas and hopeful skies. Then there was another notorious shade of blue Sheldon remembered.

He sees the Disinfection Building in Auschwitz behind his eyelids. There are the procedures of separation and surrender. Children were separated from their mothers, wives from their husbands, and the elderly from everyone. Whether they lived or died, prisoners ceded their clothes and possessions. The hair on their heads and bodies shaved, they walked naked into the shower rooms, relieved at the promise of cleanliness and some dignity after the long train rides surrounded by human filth and misery. Sheldon would watch them stare at the showerheads and wait for the water that never fell. None of them had noticed the absence of windows and drains until it was too late.

Zyklon-B would color the ceiling cerulean blue.

He'd move bodies, hour after hour, into the crematoria. Each corpse told a story that ended the same way, a death that started with excruciating pain, then convulsions, and a coup de grâce of cardiac arrest. As he worked the endless harvest of death, he'd hear the voices of the Nazi sadists Gerhard Palitzsch, Hans Aumeier, and the shrill Maximilian Grabner. The camp's commandant Rudolf Höss passed him numerous times, quiet as a shadow. The gassed were cremated, their bones collected from the drawers and thrown under a roller that crushed the remains into chalk. Every day for him was a recitation of the Mourner's Kaddish. The Gentiles might say at their funerals, 'ashes to ashes, dust to dust,' but he had lived it.

Nothing was wasted at Auschwitz. He'd seen the sacks of human hair, the pliers and teeth, the pits for those shot and dumped, and the open field of flames. The part of the camp the prisoners called Canada was where the shoes and the suitcases from the trains were stored. There was the rumor of a brothel in Block 24.

There were those who resisted. Few people knew about the prisoners who rioted at Auschwitz. The Nazis quashed the insurrection. Ala Gertner, Roza Robota, Regina Safirsztajn and Estusia Wajcblum were led to the gallows. Sheldon and the other prisoners were forced to witness their executions. Before they died, they shouted in Hebrew, 'Chazak V'amatzz' or 'Be strong and resolute.' The short-drop method of hanging was meant to be cruel and not snap their necks. The camp watched the martyrs as they writhed until the final spasm and twitch claimed them.

He sprang up, his hand to his throat.

Sheldon walked into his kitchen and grabbed the Moka. He ran the tap for water to fill up the base. He spooned out some ground coffee into the filter catch, twisted the aluminum octagon top of his Bialetti onto the base, and lit the burner for the small blue flame. He waited for the aromatic coffee. He shut the flame off before the espresso sputtered. He poured his coffee and shot back the caffeine.

In the bathroom he stropped the blade, then splashed hot water on his face. After the lather, he used the straight razor with Damascus steel on his face. He ended the ritual with a splash of cold water. He cleaned the instrument, and rinsed out his brush. He applied some sandalwood scented Taylor's After Shave Gel to his skin.

He bought a newspaper and a small pastry. On his way back to his apartment, he passed rooms and the bookshop to access the stairwell to his place. He passed the janitor's closet on the second floor, the same place where he had heard the odd noise. The dream of the camp reminded him that silence was a sin.

The workman was a bull of a man in overalls, with a rock-hard paunch, and his whiskers came in dark as soot, which made his face look dirty all the time. The man was hirsute. A mess of black hair, thick as fur curled around his shoulder straps. He reeked of sweat and hard liquor.

Numerous times Sheldon had walked past the man's walk-in on the second floor.

Today would be different. It was before the bookstore opened.

He stood in the hallway, outside the door. He heard those sounds again. Female. His hand tried the knob. The door was unlocked and he opened the door.

The sight horrified him.

There on the floorboards was the janitor on top of a young girl. Her hand clawed wood, in an attempt to escape the beast on her back. The man's body moved like an angry inchworm, as his hips thrusted into her.

Sheldon saw her legs parted, a hamstring quivered during the assault. Unaware of Sheldon behind him, deaf to the sound of the pastry bag he had dropped, Sheldon pinned the man's leg to the floor with his foot. He grabbed an overall strap, looped it around the man's throat and pulled the makeshift snare hard with all his strength. He waited until life left the man.

He rolled the rapist off his victim. She crawled out crab-like from under her attacker. A wedge of sunlight shone white across her nakedness. She scuttled to the wall and held her knees to her chest. She panted and stared wild-eyed at Sheldon. Suddenly, she lunged forward on her knees and pummeled the dead man, beating him until she was exhausted. She sobbed and heaved.

Sheldon waited until she stopped. He reassured her. He told her in German, "I won't hurt you. You need to get out of here."

She looked around and gathered her torn clothes and looked at the dead body.

"I'll take care of that," he said. "Can you stand up and move on your own?"

She nodded.

Sheldon approached her slowly and thought that the last thing this girl wanted was another man touching her. She put her shirt on. Her hands trembled as they tried to fasten what buttons were left on the blouse. The bottom half of her clothes were useless. He watched her face go pale and blank. Shock had set in. She wavered where she stood, unsure as a newborn fawn. Sheldon saw the blood trickle down her thigh.

He offered her his arm, which she pushed away. Time was critical, he told her. They had to leave, but she didn't seem to hear him. He had to force their flight from the scene. When he swooped her up in his arms, her arms wrapped themselves around his neck. He moved fast, out of the room, down the hall, and up the stairs to his room.

He took her into his bathroom and turned on both faucets to the tub. Clothes and all, he placed her in the tub and let the water surround her. Sheldon said he'd return. He ran downstairs to survey what he needed to do to dispose of the body that evening. He picked up the pastry bag.

Upstairs, he fished out a bathrobe and knocked on the bathroom door. She didn't answer, so he went inside. She held a washcloth and a bar of soap in her hands. She looked up at him; the color had returned to her face. He couldn't find any words to say to her, except, "You are safe here," in German.

Sheldon sat in the living room. He waited. He looked down at his pants and saw her blood had taken the shape of a small violet butterfly on his leg. He sat there and took in his small world that he'd have to share with another person. He had an oriental area rug, a small bookcase with a modest collection of novels from previous tenants, a square dining table against the wall with two chairs, and curtains on two windows. The rest of his kingdom consisted of a bathroom, a bedroom, and a smaller than small kitchenette.

She came out in his bathrobe. She walked the walk of someone violated.

He stood up. "My name is Sheldon. Here, please sit down."

She said nothing.

"Do you have family?"

She didn't answer.

"Do you want to stay here?"

She nodded yes.

"I can't call the police."

She held the lapels of the bathrobe tightly. She didn't look at him.

"I will take care of downstairs later tonight."

She remained silent.

"I'll go out for some food and find some clothes for you." Again, silence.

"Will you be here when I return?"

She nodded yes.

"You can lie down in the next room if you wish." He pointed to his bedroom, although she didn't look. He handed her the bag with the pastry. She held it not knowing what to do with it.

He assessed her. She was thirteen, maybe. Her hair was white, as if it hadn't decided on its color. There was some darkness in her eyebrows. Her lips were red and raw, but he didn't know whether that was from the man downstairs or not.

As he went to the door he heard a gurgle that made him look over his shoulder.

"My name is Tania."

He knew from her pronunciation that she was Russian.

And that her name meant 'fairy queen.'

Chapter Ten

The office was abuzz like a beehive.

Walker grabbed the elbow of a random secretary. "What's happening?"

"Impromptu meeting. Second door down on the left."

"Mr. Marshall has been looking for you," an analyst said, walking past him. Walker thought to ask the young man in his grip another question but he was gone. Then he saw her and she saw him. He approached her.

"Leslie, who's here?"

"Mr. Meeks and Davies. They arrived from Karlsruhe late last night."

"That's earlier than expected."

"Don't think it wasn't intentional."

"Would Davies do that to Jack?"

"I doubt it. Meeks is behind the early arrival," she said.

"Since he's with the oversight committee, he wants to show he has power?"

"Arrive a day early, and all the answers aren't inside a frame on the wall. Walk with me to the office," she said, but stopped and handed him her handkerchief. "Get rid of the perspiration, and where's your tie?"

"I threw it away. It's a long story, and thanks for the pocket square."

While he wiped away some sweat from his forehead, Leslie dusted off his shoulders with her palms and adjusted his shirt collar. It wasn't maternal and it wasn't Sis helping her brother for a date with her best friend, but it was touch he appreciated and enjoyed.

"Any advice?" he asked.

"Follow Jack's lead, and don't let Meeks get under your skin."

"I heard he has that habit. Under the skin, I mean."

"Like a tick."

"I never met the man."

"First times are memorable," she said.

"Are we still talking about Meeks?"

* * *

Mr. Meeks sat with Major General Davies across from Jack when Walker entered the room with Leslie behind him. Jack introduced Walker and mentioned that they had served together in the 36th. Meeks didn't cotton to Jack's upbeat tone and enthusiasm. He acted with all the solemnity of an auditor with a tax return. "Is he one of your best?" Mr. Meeks asked.

"I trust him with my life and—"

"Ah, a collier's faith. How charming."

General Davies winced at the idea that the man would interrupt Jack. Walker started to think that Jack would like to do to Mr. Meeks what Patton had done to that soldier suffering from battle fatigue, except Jack would slap the man harder, mean it, and never apologize.

Mr. Meeks appeared old for the job. His hair was silver, and buzzed to the scalp. His suit was gray, the foulard tie included some more gray, two stripes worth. Meeks adhered to Beau Brummel's dictum for the British gentleman on fashion; his clothes drew no attention to the man himself. If Coco Chanel advised women to remove one accessory before they left the house, Brummel advocated for less is more. Meeks was Old Guard, the careerist who lived for God and Country. The question often asked was, which country?

Meeks had served in the First World War, when intelligence was in its infancy. The twin British intelligence agencies, MI5 and 6, were formed in 1909. His military service brought him to England, and despite his birth in the American South, he became a man of the Empire, a knight-errant of the British Crown. He honed his craft and made his name in the field with a controversial operation overseas. He focused on British officers with

German relatives. After the Armistice, or some say during it, he adopted England, but nobody was sure whether she had adopted him. Meeks was, in other words, the epitome of the three Ps: Patrician, Paternalistic, and a Pain in the backside.

Everyone knew of Meeks stateside. They had no choice. The man was connected to senators, sub-committees, and numerous advisory boards. He was as ubiquitous as a mosquito on a summer day, and left people annoyed and scratching themselves in impolite places.

While Walker may have never met the man, it didn't stop Jack from expressing his bias. Jack viewed him as one of those inbred Southerners who had spent too many generations in the sun, in their seersucker suit under the magnolia trees with mint juleps. Meeks was a scion of ambition, Jack said. His people considered the name Sherman a profanity. His family went from claiming Christian virtues by day and riding out at night under white sheets to dinners with congressmen and presidents. Jack equated the man's ascendency to a dirty martini.

A secretary knocked on the door and asked for Leslie, saying that there was a delivery for her. Walker sat down. Major General Davies started the meeting.

"Mr. Meeks heads the civilian oversight committee on our operations here in Vienna. He comes to us from Washington and with the cooperation of BOB in Berlin."

Davies had used the acronym B.O.B. for Company HQ, Berlin Operating Base.

Meeks set the tone. "The Company is a continuation of Bill Donovan's OSS, and the enterprise is, as such, funded by the American taxpayer. Washington wishes to respect Company autonomy, the nature of its work, while confirming there is efficiency with monies allocated to the agency's efforts in Europe."

Leslie returned. The Major General lifted himself out of his seat to acknowledge a lady's presence. She smiled at him, while Jack stared at Meeks. Leslie carried in with her a silver tea service. She set it down. Jack's attention moved from Meeks to Davies to Walker, then to Leslie with her tray and accessories. Meeks instructed her to set the small timer for the correct steeping time.

When Leslie resumed her seat, she produced a steno pad. Walker watched her pull a pencil from over her ear and set its point down on the pad. Meeks interrupted Walker's admiration of her when he said to her, "That'll be all. Thank you."

Leslie looked surprised, turned to Jack who blinked slowly as an apology for her dismissal. She rose from her seat without a word. Davies flinched a weak smile. Walker didn't want her to go but he enjoyed watching her leave the room.

When the little bell pinged, Meeks poured his tea into a small china teacup. The men watched and waited for Meeks as he took a sip of his tea. He spoke after he seemed satisfied with the tea. "Now to the matter at hand." The man's eyes squinted as if they had spotted a fleck of lint on Walker. "Where is your necktie?"

"I didn't think there would be a meeting today."

"I see." Meeks adjusted some papers in front of him. Meeks pushed something in front of Jack, who didn't look down. "This is a list of persons of interest in Vienna who claim to have knowledge of the locations of Soviet rockets and scientists. We need to corroborate their claims."

The room was quiet. Meeks liked the sound of his own voice.

"A status on the SS officer found in the asylum, please?"

"It seems someone beat us to him," Jack said.

"Murdered?" Meeks asked.

"That appears to be the case, yes."

Leslie returned with a cup of coffee, which she placed in front of Davies. The Major General thanked her and she left.

Meeks asked, "Suspects?"

"It's an open investigation, and Walker is the lead."

"Is the IP involved?"

Jack answered. "On a need-to-know basis."

"Odd," Meeks said. "I was led to believe a former camp survivor was the lead suspect."

"Led by whom?" Jack asked.

"I read the same reports you do, Mr. Marshall."

"I reached a different conclusion about the man."

"But he is a suspect in other assassinations."

"Those events did not take place in Vienna, so they are outside of my purview. We have found no direct connection between him and the asylum."

"But the man is a vigilante," Meeks said.

"There is no proof he committed any of those assassinations."

"I see, but there is evidence the man is a homosexual."

Jack was annoyed with the schoolmaster tone of voice. "And your point is?"

The Major General sampled his coffee.

Meeks hands came together. "It's a subversive lifestyle and there's a pattern."

"A pattern for what?" Jack asked.

"First, he's a homosexual. Second, he was a collaborator with the Nazi machinery of death. According to our paperwork, he speaks Russian and other languages. For all we know he could be a Red or have communist sympathies. And there's the mystery of why he is in Vienna."

Jack couldn't resist. "Maybe he's here to learn the waltz."

Meeks' expression soured.

The Major General coughed and played the diplomat. "What I think Mr. Marshall is trying to say is that we shouldn't jump to conclusions. Homosexuals have been with us since the dawn of time, Mr. Meeks. Alexander the Great, a slew of renaissance painters. The list goes on. If you've read the report, then you would know the man had been raped."

Meeks replied. "Revenge is a motive, and what of his complicity with the Nazis?"

Jack said, "Damn hypocrites."

"Excuse me. You have something that you'd like to add, Mr. Marshall?"

"According to you, it seems that he must be guilty of something. First, he is a Nazi collaborator, then a vigilante; but wait, no, he must be a Communist because he speaks Russian, and now you say he's a homosexual, so that must mean he is a harbinger of the Apocalypse."

Davies tried to diffuse the tension before Meeks could respond. "It's no crime the man speaks Russian. Most Europeans speak more than one language."

"Point taken," Meeks said. "Is the man allied with any of the Zionist groups in Vienna? The Brits have formed a list of questionable characters."

"I bet they did," Jack said.

Meeks ignored the remark. "Does the man work for or with anyone?"

Jack answered. "We believe he acts alone."

Meeks seemed satisfied. "And what about your man Whittaker?"

"What about him?" Jack said.

"I understand that he is AWOL."

"He is in the field, and that often entails days without contact."

"Isn't that irregular, the lack of communication, Mr. Marshall?"

Walker clenched his eyes, and Davies shifted in his seat.

"I resent the implication, Mr. Meeks."

"I'm stating a fact, Mr. Marshall, and request an explanation."

"The fact is you are out of your depth, Mr. Meeks, and I dislike the insinuation that I don't keep my house in order. With all due respect, you're a civilian, and you had your day in the sun in the first war. The field of intelligence is different now, and the rules of engagement have changed. Vienna is not the trenches, or No Man's Land in some godforsaken countryside."

Jack's voice was calm as he delivered the verbal one-two jab to the teeth with a hook to the liver. Meeks showed no reaction to the blows or where they landed.

"Mr. Marshall, the fact is Whittaker is missing."

"He'll contact me when the time is right."

"Ah, there's that faith again," Meeks said.

Jack said, "You used the phrase 'collier's faith' earlier. I know what those words mean. I learned them from a man under me, a private from the coal mining country of West Virginia. He witnessed the Matewan Massacre, Mr. Meeks. He taught this officer before you something you'd do well to understand and respect. Rank does not a leader make. A leader is someone men believe in enough that they'd go to the gates of Hell for you, and they trust the order, even if they don't understand it because they know you don't think of them as nothing more than canaries sent down the mineshaft. I'm obligated to honor that faith and trust, so I stand by what I said about Whittaker. The man will contact me when the time is right."

Davies cut in. "Can we move on to other matters? The list you gave Jack, perhaps."

Jack picked up the piece of paper Meeks had put across the table. "I'll review this."

"We'll meet again and you can provide me with a status on your progress." Meeks stood up. He requested that Leslie have the tea service returned to his hotel. There was silence after Meeks quit the room, and the click of the door was a memory. Davies took out a pack of cigarettes, tamped the box, and shook a smoke loose. He placed the cigarette between his lips and Walker leaned over with a lit match. The General took in a breath and exhaled a long languorous plume of smoke.

"Good thing you didn't wring his neck, Jack. I know you were tempted. Am I wrong?"

"More like piss on his tea leaves. I'd like to know how he knew Whittaker was missing? Did you tell him?"

"I did not." Davies tapped some ash into a clean ashtray. "It's a curious question, indeed, since it's not in any of the status reports. I should go."

Davies left. Jack stared at the tea service. Both he and Walker shared the same thought without saying it: Who else knows about their office after the hotel delivered the silver set?

Chapter Eleven

L eslie phoned Walker. "Can we meet and talk?" she said.

The low whisper behind her voice sounded as if she were stuck in a telephone booth at Schwab's Pharmacy, upset, and the regulars at the counter were attentive to her every syllable.

Walker checked his watch, 2000 hours, 8pm in civilian time. He remembered that he'd been meaning to get a new wrist-strap, upgrade from lizard to alligator. "We're talking now."

"I meant in person, Walker," she said, calm and polite.

"In person?"

"Perhaps for a drink?"

He treaded between reserved and enthusiastic. "Where?"

"The usual place?"

"Perfect," she said.

He tried not to read the slight uptick in her voice as something that she could count as victory. She had asked, he had answered, and now he had to go to her, which was how he remembered all his encounters with women.

The 'usual place' was a small café the office used for drinks to celebrate the end of each week. It was two blocks from Walker's place. The polite thing to do, he thought, was to get there before her since a lady alone was an invitation for the wolves with lonely hearts. Austrians were not known for being ardent lovers, but that never stopped the predatory male. They agreed on a time and hung up.

* * *

Walker ordered himself an iced wine, eiswein, which earned him a queer look from the barkeep. It was rare that a man would order sweet wine as a drink. For Walker, it indulged his sweet tooth and satisfied a curiosity. He wanted to see what the Viennese were doing with the Riesling grape and compare it to his memory to what the Canadians had done with the Vidal blanc varietal when he visited America's rooftop neighbor for some skiing last year before he accepted Jack's invitation to join the Company.

He took a sip. Not bad, he thought, and looked around the establishment. A gust of cold air swept in with Leslie. He headed to a table and she followed his lead. He offered her a cigarette.

"No, thank you." She looked around, as if she was worried.

"What's on your mind, Leslie?"

"Thinking."

"I try to keep that to a minimum after sundown."

She started to say something, but packed her sentence away when a waiter stepped up to their table for her order. She ordered herself schnapps. He noticed her ensemble of tawny suit, tailor-made, an incandescent white blouse, and the entire package tied off with a scarf of raw silk around her neck. She'd grown her hair out. She varied how she'd wear it, sometimes with a part or sometimes combed forward. Nobody knew her true color.

The schnapps came. She took a sip but it wasn't long before the glass started to sweat and leave a ring on the table. He paced the ice wine to avoid the head rush. His mouth tasted sweet and cold. She came out with it when he was in mid-swallow.

"Meeks is at the Hotel Sacher, along with his precious silver tea set."

"British territory. Why are you surprised? The man is an Anglophile."

"He does put on quite the show to make everyone forget he's from the South." She drank more of her schnapps. "There's no reason for a man to be ashamed of where he's from. You don't care if someone is from that part of the country, do you?"

"As a rule, no, but it's hard to not think stereotypes."

"You mean, discrimination and the Klan."

"I was thinking of stronger words, like racism and lynching. Add in Jim

Crow, and poverty and corruption. The South is the only place I know where you can find a snake on both land and water. What's really on your mind, Leslie."

"Meeks."

"Sore that he asked you to leave the room?"

She nodded. It was an honest yes. She then looked away, which said everything about her wounded pride. Meeks had dismissed her. Jack had too, but carelessly. Meeks was deliberative and dismissive. He imagined she was upset that Davies, who didn't come to her defense. Davies had, after all, lobbied hard for her spot on Jack's team. Walker wanted to reach across the table and touch her fingers as a gesture of compassion. He didn't.

He offered solace and rationalization, instead.

"I doubt Meeks is aware of your accomplishments before you came to Vienna."

"Don't be so sure of that," she said. "I wouldn't be surprised if he didn't read the files on every single person in the office."

"And it stings that he thinks of you as a secretary?"

"Most men do, even if they're aware of a woman's service record." Her hand on the glass. "He asked about Whittaker when I wasn't in the room, didn't he?"

The way she asked the question was first-rate acting. He let the question hang in the air. He'd let her wiggle in the web some.

"Meeks said Whittaker was AWOL, and implied Jack didn't run a tight shop."

"But you're not buying the subscription?" she asked.

"Meeks is planting the seed that Whittaker is up to no good, or gone native."

"And what does Jack think?"

"You could ask Jack yourself."

"But I'm asking you."

"Jack is loyal to Whittaker. Their service together, and all."

"You said 'their' instead of 'our.' Have reservations?"

"Whittaker has his faults. We all do. I'll leave it at that, Leslie."

After a small sip, she said. "Do you think the war changed Whittaker?"

"The war changed everybody and everything, Leslie. I shouldn't have to tell you that. Were those changes enough to make Whittaker have a change of heart? No, I don't think so. If Whittaker has gone radio silent, it's for a reason. What do you think?"

Leslie flushed. "I don't think you can ever know someone. Meeks worries me."

"Why is that?"

"Which part?" she asked. "Not knowing someone or Meeks?"

"Lady's choice."

"Meeks is here to make sure everything is done by the book."

"And what book is that? I thought we were all making it up as we go along. The Company is new."

"But not inexperienced," she said.

"True, but the operations and tempo have changed. You're the analyst, Leslie, so explain the scene before us."

"What scene?"

"Take your pick. Vienna. Whittaker. Meeks."

A hard gulp of ice wine, and the sugar hit his brain.

"You want my analysis, is that it, Walker? Where do I start?"

"Start with me."

"You? Are you sure about that?" Leslie toyed with the stem of her glass. She rotated it with the long fingers of her right hand. "You want Jack to do all your thinking for you. He's the superior and you're the subordinate. It's comfortable for you. You don't know what you want and you don't trust your own mind. How am I doing?"

"Ouch," he said, "That's harsh, don't you think?"

"But fair, and there's an upside. You two are stronger together. It's like algebra, when you have to solve an equation with two variables. Substitution is required for the solution. Take out Jack, put in Walker."

"In one analogy and two sentences, I'm both insulted and complimented," Walker said.

"It's not for lack of intelligence," she said.

"Insulted again."

"It's all about passion. Jack has his, Meeks has his, but you haven't found yours yet."

"And I'm in Vienna because Jack called, is that?" Walker looked away.

"Jack gave you a purpose, but this isn't you, Walker."

"Are we done, Anna Freud? Let's get back to you, Meeks, and Whittaker."

She gripped the wineglass by the stem. "Meeks is politics."

"And what happened to Sheldon, to millions of others, that wasn't politics?"

Without looking up from her drink, she said, "A personal question for you, Walker."

"We're not personal already?"

"Why'd you name your service weapon Grable?"

"Long story."

Walker could feel his heartbeat. She had worked him up, and now she toyed with him.

"I see. You don't want to embarrass yourself."

"How does your question about her embarrass me?" he asked.

"I grew up with brothers. Men name things that they are attached to, or should I say things attached to them."

"It's nothing like that," he said.

"Then how is it?"

"I kept a small picture of Betty Grable on me in the service. The guys teased me."

"I assume you're fond of blondes and legs."

"It wasn't the reason why I had the photo. There was a note written on the back of the photo, which meant a lot to me."

"From?"

"Peggy."

"Your sweetheart?"

Walker nodded. Leslie hunted for a cigarette. "Why, Walker, you're a romantic."

"It's curable."

"Strange that a girl would send you off with a picture of another woman."

Her mouth was nice. She wore her lipstick well.

"It was a joke between us. We went out on a date, saw a film, and she kidded me about having to compete with a film star. It was all in good fun. Anyway, the world has spun several times on its axis since."

She looked down at her drink. "Sounds nice to have had that kind of love. An affair of the heart. The French have a word for it."

"I have a name for it, too, but it isn't polite."

"Meeks is a dog after a bone, and Whittaker is on his list."

"And there's a non-sequitur," Walker said. "Relax, Leslie. Whittaker will show up. He always does. He's always been something of a wild card."

"How was he a wild card?"

"Whittaker likes women and gambling. He's not very good with either of them."

Leslie shot a look at him. She seemed offended.

"My turn for a non-sequitur," he said. "You said earlier that you grew up with brothers. It's the first time you've shared something personal. Where are you from?"

"Shaker Heights. I ought to go."

"Was it something I said?"

"No, I'm tired, and it's been a long day. Would you tell me if you heard from Whittaker?" He said that he would. She reached into her purse and took out a pen and a piece of paper and scribbled something. She handed the note to him.

"What is this?" he asked.

"My phone number."

"For when I hear from Whittaker?" he said and slipped her number into his pocket.

"That, and if you need to talk. The next round of drinks is on me."

He thought about having coffee, but he decided against it. He didn't need the caffeine to stay up. He knew he would be up all night thinking.

Chapter Twelve

Jack eyed the parcel of land, the Wienzeile, over the Wien River.

He'd bought himself an apple and stopped to watch the crowd. Fruit sellers manned stalls, customers roamed, lingered, smelled produce, touched and assessed the quality of materials and goods in the market square. People bought, haggled, and paid for fruits, meats, and other items.

Jack wiped his hands of stickiness with a handkerchief from his back pocket. He thought back to people-watching with other Company men at Foggy Bottom in DC. Thousands of miles away, their meetings ended with a generous intake of Heurich beer.

Jack was a witness to the Vienna that wasn't in any reports. He'd seen how the Viennese survived the Russian occupation, the rapes, robberies, and other crimes. There was that gallows joke that Vienna could stomach another war but could never survive a second liberation.

He located Sheldon's place of employment a short distance from the Naschmarkt. If the place was a front, it was well thought-out and clever. He'd thought about how his own office enjoyed a similar cover, until Sheldon and Meeks compromised it. First, Sheldon appeared unannounced, and then Meeks had someone from his hotel deliver his precious tea service. He decided to step into Sheldon's world, to return the favor.

"May I help you, sir," the salesman said in polite German.

Sheldon approached, placed his hand on a shoulder. "I'll take it from here," he said. Sheldon's hand pointed to a display. "Allow me to show you around. Looking for something particular?"

"The latest in menswear, please."

"You must know that Vienna isn't known for fashion."

"I know the war has knocked Paris off her pedestal, but I have to start somewhere."

Sheldon walked over to a carousel with Jack. His hand worked through some selections. The manager had retreated to the back of the store but observed the sales floor. Jack tried to look interested. "Show me the latest from the States."

"Men's fashion there is suits in dark blue and brown, and lots of gray flannel. Ties are slimmer, hats are with a narrower brim, though, I'm happy to say, the fedora remains a popular staple. Little in the way of style overall, so let's see what we have here."

The hooks scraped the metal dowel as he pulled some hangers.

"If the French are quiet for now," Jack said. "What about the British?"

"The young set favor an Edwardian look of brocade vests, narrow trousers, jackets trimmed with velvet, and suede shoes. It's not a look for you, Mr. Marshall."

"Agreed. I'm no longer young and never an Anglophile."

"No tea at the Hotel Sacher for you then?"

"Advice on something casual?"

Sheldon lifted a bright Hawaiian shirt from the rack. The audacious pattern lit up Jack's eyes. Sheldon held up a Kahala to Jack's face. Jack asked, "Obnoxious, don't you think?"

"As a neon sign," Sheldon said. "Bold for all the wrong reasons. This shirt is what everybody thinks when they see an American." Sheldon returned the loud example to the display.

"I don't know about all Americans, but I'm interested in one in particular."

Sheldon retrieved a pack of cigarettes from his pocket. "I'm due for a break, join me?"

"I didn't know you smoked."

Outside, Sheldon handed him the pack of cigarettes. The cardboard wasn't crunched up, the edge of the wrapping wasn't torn and the tobacco wasn't tamped.

Jack handed the pack back to him. "Almost had me fooled."

Sheldon indicated a spot, away from the store. "What can I do for you, Mr. Marshall?"

"I'd like to know where Whittaker is?"

"I told you what I knew when we last spoke." Sheldon's fingers fidgeted with the cigarette. He didn't light it. "What is the latest you have on the man?"

"Apartment looks like a bender minus the booze, the women, or smokes. From where I'm standing that makes you the last person to have spoken with him. Unless some other information falls my way, you're all I've got at the moment."

"I am a suspect then?"

"Afraid so."

"Wish I could be of help to you, Mr. Marshall, but I was honest with you."

"I wish I could believe you, Sheldon. One way or the other I'll find the truth."

"Will you?"

Jack didn't know whether it was a question, a threat, or a simple statement.

"You Americans are forever optimistic," Sheldon said. "I've been truthful with you. Whittaker came to see me. He tried to be persuasive but *that* didn't work out the way Whittaker had planned."

"You don't say?" Jack replied.

"I didn't harm Whittaker, Mr. Marshall. What's my motive?"

"So, he walked out the door upright?"

"May I offer you some advice, Mr. Marshall?" Jack said yes without saying the word. "For hundreds of years people never questioned why things fell to the ground when they dropped them."

"Are we talking about gravity here?" Jack said.

"More like, cause and effect. Action and reaction."

"Careful, Sheldon. Don't get under my skin. You might not like the way I scratch."

"We all have something to lose or gain. You do, Walker does, but what does Whittaker have to lose or gain? Answer that question and you might have an idea why he disappeared."

"Do you have something to lose?"

Sheldon wrote something on a piece of paper. He handed it to Jack.

"What's this?"

"A name. The place is a café. Go there around 10am, tomorrow."

Jack read the address. "This is in the Soviet section."

"You'll find him in the back of the room." Sheldon reached into his breast pocket and retrieved his wallet. He opened the leather billfold and handed what was inside to Jack. "Put this on the table when you see him. And a final word of advice: don't go in armed, and whatever you do, don't act like John Wayne."

"Into the lion's den, then?" Jack said. He held a handsome gold coin in his hand. The GERB, the Russian coat of arms, the two-headed eagle, was face up and on the back, the numeral five above some Cyrillic text and the date, 1885. "What is this?" he asked.

"A five-ruble coin, imperial, and rare."

"And this is significant to my date at the café?"

"It says he should trust you, so don't lie to him."

"And what can this fellow do for me?"

"He can provide you information."

"Can't I just send Walker?" Jack asked.

"Walker is a man who needs a weapon to deal with the world. That's not a criticism of the man, but it's a very American way of dealing with life."

"Anything else?"

"This man that you are meeting would want to talk to *the* American, not *an* American."

"This man knows who I am?"

"Everyone. who is someone in Vienna, knows Jack Marshall."

"And here I was, thinking I wasn't special."

"They have a name for you here."

"What is it?"

"Equus."

Jack thought back to his Latin. Masculine. Second declension. "I'm a horse?"

"In Vienna, you're a very special kind of horse, Mr. Marshall."

"Wonderful. Let's go back inside. You can help me with some clothes."

Sheldon took measurements for a double-breasted suit. Jack chose four buttons instead of six, no shoulder pads, and the trousers would remain long though less full, because he had those long legs of a horse, and he chose against type, navy blue instead of army green.

Chapter Thirteen

She slept in Sheldon's bed. Sunlight streamed in through a window, his pillow crushed in a caress meant as a cushion between her and Vienna outside. She was wearing one of his long shirts. Those first days were the first rest she had known in days, weeks, possibly months.

Sheldon slept in his living room. He delivered her meals. She ate little. Her eyes opened when she heard him at the door. She didn't smile but she was grateful to see him. He crossed the room with a large cup of fresh coffee and frothed milk, topped off with some fresh cocoa on the white snowcap. She noticed that when Sheldon covered the distance between the door and the bed, he moved with an ethereal silence. The floorboards didn't creak, and the china cup on the saucer didn't shiver, titter or teeter.

She pulled herself up in bed with the duvet, rested herself against the pillows she propped up behind her. Coffee cup and saucer in her hands, he sat on the edge of the bed.

"How are you feeling?"

"Good, I guess. About downstairs."

"It's taken care of. Is there anything I can do for you?" She shook her head. "Do you have family I can," and stopped when she turned away. He had asked her once before. "I understand," he said.

"Do you?"

"I have no one," he said. "My family was exterminated."

"My mother is dead, and I ran away with my father when the police came for us."

"Which police?" Sheldon asked.

"The secret police in Budapest. He was a journalist."

"Words are dangerous."

"He said it was only a matter of time. He sent me here ahead of him, and we were supposed to meet here, but I guess they arrested him first. I don't know." She set aside the coffee and pulled her knees to her chest. She rested her chin on them.

"You don't think he escaped Budapest?"

"No," she said, and he asked why. She said, "He told me, that there was this man who would bump into him. He'd say to my father, "Comrade, how is your health?""

To Sheldon, the tactic sounded like something the SMERSH would do. Whatever her father committed to the page had earned him Stalin's disapproval.

"About downstairs," Sheldon said. She pressed her knees tighter into her chest. "How did you come to be with him? I ask because I need to know, so if anyone comes looking for him they don't find you."

"He seemed nice at first." She turned her head away and grabbed the pillow and put her face into it. He wanted to touch her but he knew that he shouldn't. After a protracted silence she lifted her head up. "Sorry." Her eyes looked puffy.

"I had to bring it up. It's a matter of safety, yours and mine."

"I won't cause you any trouble, I promise. That man didn't know my father. He was someone I thought I could trust and stay with for a little while, before I figured out where I was going to go next. I could apply to the Displaced Person's Camp, claim refugee status, and take my chances."

"No, that isn't necessary, and unwise."

Sheldon knew the Soviets had spies among the refugees, looking for people like her father. He told her, "If they find you, it's off to a labor camp if you're lucky. For a young and attractive girl like you, the outcome is much worse."

The frightened expression on her face made him stop.

"Can I stay with you?" she said. "I won't be much trouble." She wiped away her tears with the sleeve of his nightshirt. "I could keep this place up for you." There was that brief smile, a ring of confidence in her voice. "And I could be nice to you."

Sheldon understood bargaining. "That won't be necessary."

She tensed up. "You can learn to like me, can't you?"

"It isn't that."

"Then what is it?"

He didn't answer her. He realized he had no idea how young girls passed their time. There were so many holes in his life. "All I ask is that you keep quiet while you're here. Please, stay. I don't want you to leave. You don't have to cook or clean. I will help you the best I can."

"Why? Why do you want to help me?"

Sheldon stood up. He had a world of answers for her but not enough time to explain any of them. A weariness crept into his voice. "Because I understand more than you think."

Chapter Fourteen

Jack stood on a footbridge and took in the view of Leopoldstadt. He reread Sheldon's note.

The Russians occupied the once walled-in Jewish ghetto before him. In the past, the Jewish community had funded the Thirty Years War for the Habsburgs, before Leopold I and his beautiful wife Margaret Theresa of Spain had them kicked out on the nonsense charge of spying for the Turks and then for blasphemy against the Virgin Mother. The Jews would remain exiled until the 1848 Revolutions returned them to Vienna.

In 1941, Hitler had initiated the deportations of Jews from Leopoldstadt. The ethnic population at the time numbered a few thousand and by the war's end, a few hundred. The Wannsee Conference took place the following year. The likes of Reinhard Heydrich and his cohorts gathered at a lakeside villa to discuss what to do with European Jewry. While Adolph Eichmann walked Heydrich's dogs outside, his superiors met inside and outlined die Endlösung der Judenfrage, or the Final Solution to the Jewish question. In one hundred minutes, fifteen men decided the fate of millions over breakfast, cigars, and cognac. Jack had read the minutes to the meeting that a secretary had hidden in a wall inside the residence. The Company marked the document TOP SECRET and filed it away. Like the film footage taken at the camps in the aftermath of liberation, the world was not ready to view the monsters that had dared to walk in daylight.

Jack accepted Sheldon's advice when he left his room at the Hotel Bristol. He would not look like an American. The absence of a sidearm on his person made him feel as if he'd forgotten to use a towel after his shower.

The one thing that delighted him most here was the sight of chestnut trees along the Hauptallee. The rest of what he saw were reminders of the war, especially near the porcelain factory where there were two Flaktürme, or anti-aircraft towers that the Luftwaffe had used against Allied Forces. The Combat Tower, in particular, had holes for eight 128 mm guns and thirty-two 20-mm guns. Now, pigeons infected them.

He found the café.

Jack touched the coin in his pocket while he searched the room for his mark. He walked towards the man he determined was Sheldon's contact. Two men in dark suits stopped him. Jack held up the coin for their boss to see. Something was said in Russian, and two oversized hands frisked him before they released him. Jack approached the table, placed the coin on it, and sat down.

"My name is Jack Marshall."

"I know who you are, Comrade."

Jack made a quick study of the man. Broad shouldered, clean-shaven, his hair tight, eyes blue and above placid cheekbones. Jack's guest ordered two drinks.

"Are you an officer?" Jack asked.

"Why do you ask?"

"The way you asked for water says you're used to giving orders."

"I was with the Fifth Guards Tank Army under Pavel Rotmistrov."

"Vilnius wasn't good for Rotmistrov."

"Nor for me either, and now I am here."

"Vienna is your punishment?" Jack asked.

"My superiors have a sense of humor. Why did you bring this coin?"

"Proof that I can be trusted, and because I need information."

Jack paused. How much to reveal required experience, the kind that Walker lacked.

"The man who gave me this coin believes you can help me find one of my men. I have a picture of him in my breast pocket, but I don't want to reach into my pocket. I'd hate for there to be any misunderstandings."

"Retrieve your photo." The man raised his hand to let his bodyguard know it was okay.

From his pocket Jack produced a small military-issue photograph of Whittaker.

The Russian reviewed the picture. "I've seen this face."

"Tell me when and where you've seen him."

The man put a finger on the coin. "Do you know what this is?"

"I was told it was rare and royal."

"What if I told you that there was another coin, similar but rarer?"

"Only if it helps me find my man Whittaker."

The Russian officer explained that the successor to Alexander I was his brother Constantine, but he abdicated and Nikolai I ruled instead. Legend had it that the royal minter created a silver Constantine ruble before the abdication. When Alexander II assumed power in 1855, he was presented a box that held five Constantine rubles. The czar kept one coin for himself, gave one to the Hermitage, and made gifts of coins three and four. A fifth coin was lost to history, as was a sixth, the minter's personal copy. The sixth coin was considered priceless.

Jack listened, absorbed the history lesson.

"And where does Whittaker figure in this story?"

"Your friend Whittaker joined a group of men in search of the sixth coin."

"Are any of these men former Nazis?"

"Not for me to say, but your Whittaker is a gambler with debts. Tell me about the man who gave you this coin?"

Jack noticed that one of the man's hands was scarred from a hideous burn.

"A round came into the tank and bounced around the walls, killing the rest of the men."

"Sorry to hear that, but you survived," Jack said.

"I survived three such attacks. In your army that would qualify a man to be discharged, but in Russia it earns you a shot of vodka, maybe a medal, then another tank."

"Can you help me locate Whittaker?"

"First, let me ask you a question. Why does the man with the coin want to help you? You could have had him interrogated without anyone knowing it."

Jack knew each of the foreign powers in the city could have kidnapped Sheldon and taken simple ingredients, such as a small room, a light, a chair, and a table and used them to torment him for hours, and that was before they turned serious with a telephone book, a bucket of water, a copper wire, and a generator to expedite the conversation.

"I saw no need to do that to the man, like there was no need for me to have someone come down here and collect you for a chat," Jack said.

"I'm not afraid of Americans."

"Maybe you should be," Jack replied.

The general smiled. "Like most of my countrymen, I'm too busy being afraid of Stalin."

A bodyguard returned with two small glasses and a plate of pickled cucumbers and mushrooms. He set the drinks and plate on the table.

"This is horilka. Gogol called it the demon's drink."

The man raised his small glass so Jack did likewise. They clinked glasses and tipped their drinks back. A scalding heat burned Jack's throat and water ran from his eyes. He thought his tears would sizzle on his skin. Jack reached for a slice of green on the plate as a relief against the fury.

"I'll look for your friend." The general pushed the Constantine forward. "As for this coin, return it to our mutual friend. You must be honored that he entrusted it with you."

Jack dropped the coin back into his pocket. "Why do you say that?"

"Because that coin can buy safe passage for one, out of Vienna. The question for him, as it is for most Jews today, is how to answer the riddle of die Heimat."

"Thought the German homeland was der Vaterland?" Jack asked.

The general focused his eyes on Jack for a long second and then shook his head.

Jack said, "Am I wrong?"

"Heimat is more than a place, Mr. Marshall. It's a feeling, of home and belonging."

Jack thanked the Russian with the blue eyes who had fought at Kursk and Vilnius but whose name he still did not know.

Chapter Fifteen

A recent rain had glazed the streets.

Walker was thinking about *it*. Should he or shouldn't he and would she or wouldn't she when he finally said, "The hell with it," and called Leslie.

She gave him the green light and told him that he should head over to her place later.

He had started the day on the Hauptuni campus, then made his way to Haydnhaus, wondering whether or not it was true that Napoleon had put down straw on Kleine Steingasse to stifle the hoof beats of his cavalry in honor of Papa Haydn. Two blocks later on Mariahilfer Strasse he decided that he would visit the Spittelberg Quarter.

The five streets between Siebensterngasse and Burgasse make up the Quarter where Leslie lived. It was his first time to her place. When he arrived, he found the neighborhood more run down than he'd expected. It was getting dark, but he had Grable.

Walker found her apartment among some fallen baroque and Biedermeier houses. Biedermeier architecture up close was tasteless and indicative of the schlock the world had sunken to after the Congress of Vienna. The city at the time was the arch-reactionary capital of Europe. With Napoleon gone, Metternich arrived, and the clock turned back. She said she would meet him downstairs and they would walk to a restaurant.

The Quarter was alive with activity. Walker caught glimpses of nocturnal figures in the alleyways. He heard a glass bottle break. A prostitute stepped out into the light to see whether he was a prospect. He saw the white flash of a thigh, heard a whistle out of the darkness. Glassy eyes, lusty, sleepy eyes, and eyes hungry for money watched him.

He picked up his pace until he found her behind the glass of the door to her lobby, waiting for him. Leslie was in heels and snug dress, under a fashionable coat. She looked nice. He wanted to compliment her, but didn't because he thought he'd sound stupid.

They arrived at the place she'd chosen. From the nods she received Walker presumed that she was a regular. Not quite the café in the Viennese style, the establishment was an Austrian interpretation of a French bistro. A tall man pulled out a chair for her. Walker fetched his own. Menus came next. The food was French, and that meant more time for preparation and conversation.

Walker placed his napkin on his lap. "Glad you came out this evening."

"I owed you."

"You owed me a drink. This is dinner. That's a loan with substantial interest."

"Try not to overthink so much, Walker." She reviewed her menu, eyes downcast. "Decide on something?"

"Steak au poivre with a glass of red wine. You?"

Her eyes did a fast review with what he presumed was a familiar menu. "Quail stuffed with apples and sage for me." She turned the menu over for the wine list. "And a glass of white wine."

Leslie placed their orders in German. They enjoyed a good half hour of inconsequential small talk about Vienna, Mozart, and Beethoven before Walker circled the conversation back around to where he wanted. "So if Jack and I are algebra—what does that make you?"

The corners of her lips lifted. "Quick to bait my pride, are we?" She took a sip of the white wine that the waiter delivered to the table. "You want me to continue with the comparison?"

"It's your analogy." He enjoyed their abstract game of flirtation, along with his wine.

"Calculus," she said.

"Calculus?"

"It's philosophical."

"And Meeks, I imagine he is algebra?"

A waiter placed the order of steak in front of Walker. He waited until after the man delivered her quail for her answer. Leslie started in on her bird with knife and fork. "Meeks is emblematic of a different approach altogether."

"If you ask me, he is proof that civilians are best left out of operations."

"It's not a military operation, Walker."

"Nor is it measured in dollar and cents, the way his committee thinks." Walker checked the doneness of the steak with his steak knife. "How is your quail?"

"Excellent," she said. "Politicians understand as much, about money, but this is unprecedented territory, which is why they picked a military man."

"Former military, and his war and the tactics used then are antiquated. It's like that saying, don't bring a knife to a gunfight. Unprecedented, like you said."

"Few woman served in his day, and I'm a woman, so does that make my presence inappropriate?"

"Your record speaks for itself." Walker put down his knife and fork. He picked up his red wine. "This is unchartered territory, and there's a steep learning curve. Jack and I have discussed this numerous times." Leslie placed her glass emphatically on the table. He glanced up from the meat on his plate. "Did I say something wrong?"

"The point is you talk to Jack."

"Jack would talk to you. He respects you."

"It's not the same thing, Walker. I am a woman. It's no secret that Jack wasn't enthusiastic about taking me on. Davies had to soften the leather for that to happen."

"But it did happen. Past history."

"Tell yourself that enough times, and you might believe it."

"Why do I feel I am tasting my foot instead of this steak?"

"The point is no matter what's my service jacket says, I am a woman. Society uses women, reminds them to know their place, or otherwise destroys them. I gladly did my part during the war and I did it well, but I don't want to return to what is expected of me."

"I get it, you're a woman."

"All I am saying is that there's a softer boundary between men, you and Jack, whereas for women, there's a brick wall, especially in our line of work. With Meeks, its worse."

Walker said, "I didn't forget about the tea service."

"You know what I think he can do with his precious silver set. Meeks presents a bigger problem for you, Jack, and Davies."

"Because of the committee they report to?" Walker asked.

"Whoever reads his report will hold you and Jack responsible, so my advice to you and Jack is to find a way to outthink and outmaneuver Meeks. I'd do it fast, if I were you."

* * *

It was another walk, this time to her place.

"Want me to walk you up?" he asked Leslie.

"Do you want to?"

"I asked, didn't I?"

"You know, we're not teenagers anymore."

Her smile could have taught Bacall a lesson in seduction. They came to her door, and though he might've left school long ago, the anxiety as how to end the night with her was on him. Although she extended the invitation, he felt the pressure of having to make the first move, and the idea of rejection would be humiliating. A handshake seemed rude, and 'good night,' cowardly.

Leslie turned her key in the door to her apartment when a tabby darted out and circled her feet. The cat looked up, emitted a plaintive meow that suggested either starvation or neglect. Walker watched Leslie stroke and mutter baby talk to the feline.

The cat went inside with her.

He'd become tired after he saw the cat, and it wasn't the good kind of tired.

Chapter Sixteen

That damn cat.

Walker wanted to wish it all away but couldn't. Walker reclined on his bed, a young man with old worries on his mind. Sleep was harder for him than an honest answer from city hall on the shortest day of the year. He couldn't get the cat out of his head.

The feline at the door had surprised him like a riptide at the beach. He had enjoyed himself until that moment when an unexpected current sucked him into an ocean of emotions, where he was sure to drown, while everyone on the shore was oblivious to his predicament.

Leslie was different from Peggy, but if the thought of another heartbreak was a Hollywood cliché, the cat was Cagney with claws and teeth. The critter had the same color fur as the hairs on the dead Nazi's dress slacks at the Narrenturm. A coincidence, no doubt, since there had to be thousands of cats in Vienna, but the one he saw at her feet was one that wouldn't leave his imagination.

He stared at the stark ceiling, an insomniac who hoped for sleep and the simple life. He wished that he could hide his money in a coffee can, like his parents had before the war. He wished he had four walls, American-made, somewhere off Main Street. He wished he had the bachelor's solitude and the GI Bill. All he asked for were two square meals, a Murphy bed, and an icebox stocked with Falstaff beer. He wouldn't mind the routine of the boys over on Friday night for cards and cigars, the radio on in the background.

He punched the pillow for a soft spot.

The phone rang. The sound sent a chill through his self-pity. He stared at it. The phone rang again. He picked up the receiver, but the voice on the other end already knew he had picked up. Before the receiver that weighed a thousand pounds touched his ear, he heard, "Meet me at the Hotel Sacher."

Chapter Seventeen

Walker walked into the Café Sacher.

Jack sat at a table, coffee in transit to his lips. He had a plate of some decadent tooth decay in front of him. Walker ignored the dark wood panels, the rich red velvet, the glint of gold from the lamp holders, and the marble tabletops. He did notice the army of steel stands with their little flags for menus all around the room.

A waiter returned with the order that Jack had placed for Walker. On the plate before him was a cone filled with chocolate mousse. The drink that accompanied it was called a Fiaker. Walker lifted up the coffee and the whiff said that the morning's ordinance carried one shot of rum.

"We have several problems on hand," Jack said.

"Am I one of them?"

Jack's forehead wrinkled. "Why would you say that?"

"Because I have no idea what the hell I'm doing here."

Jack's fork was midway between his dish and mouth. "Don't come apart on me now."

Emboldened by the rum, Walker asked, "Of all places to meet, the Sacher?"

"I want us to be seen."

Walker tasted a forkful of the chocolate confection, a dessert that he had to admit was worth getting out of bed for.

"Walker?"

"Sorry, but this is incredible. Seen by whom?"

"The British."

"You mean Meeks. What inspired this strategy?"

"That silver tea service of his."

"I was more interested as to how Sheldon knew where the office was. Everyone seems to know more than we do, Jack, and it's worrisome. We've interviewed scores of Nazis, former SS, Wehrmacht, and we still don't know if any of them told us the truth."

Jack reached for a paper next to him. He turned the periodical around for Walker to see the lead story. "This has the British interested in us. Someone has bumped the ante."

Walker skimmed the text. His face turned somber. A simple parsing of the German unveiled the details. The lead UN negotiator in Jerusalem had been assassinated the day before.

"Don't tell me someone in MI6 thinks we're behind it," Walker said.

"Whatever they think, it's a serious setback for the Brits."

What Walker had read played out in his imagination as if it had been a movie on the silver screen. The Swede's chauffeur drove the vehicle into Zion Guini Square, where the tires were shot out with machine guns. The assassins then sprayed the car, killing the negotiator in the backseat. A French officer, who tried to defend the politician, died in the ambush.

Walker asked, "Any word as to why the man was targeted?"

"He suggested that Jews and Arabs share Jerusalem."

"Is that all?" Walker set down his cup of coffee and apologized for the sarcasm.

Jack steamrolled past it. "He also suggested that the British and American governments should oversee the repatriation of Arabs. The Lehi claimed responsibility, and they have alleged the negotiator worked for the British."

"Did he?"

"Does it matter?" Jack included a shrug with his answer. "What matters is the Brits have their eyes on everything that moves in Vienna, especially refugees."

Walker sampled more of the dessert, "You said problems when I sat down. What else?"

"The ribbons in our office; they're gone."

"All of them?" Walker asked.

"All of them."

A ritual at the close of each business day at American embassies around the world was the collection of all the typewriter ribbons used in every office. Every typewriter was numbered, and their spools, cataloged and inventoried, and then all the items were stored in a safe overnight. A marine detail performed the tasks. Jack's office was no different. Everybody pretended they didn't know the ribbon men were Marines. They might've been in plain clothes, but their haircuts made them as obvious as bouncers at the opera.

Every communication, every progress note, every report from Jack's office was missing.

Jack pulled out a xerograph, the latest technology from the lab they used, from his pocket and pushed it across the table toward Walker. "Recognize that?"

Walker looked at it. "This is a copy of that piece of paper I found at Whittaker's. Someone figure out what these numbers mean?"

"No, but the writing matches Leslie's."

"That's ridiculous. This is nothing but numbers here, Jack. You can't make a match on numbers alone."

"The lab experts tell me it's a match."

"Then they're wrong. I'm telling you, Jack, this can't be right."

"You need to stay objective, Walker."

"I am objective, Jack. This is Leslie we are talking about."

"That's the point. It's Leslie. Look, it might not be as bad as we think. All this suggests is that she is somehow tied to that money you found in the tank. Suspicion falls harder on Whittaker for it, and the rest of what you found in his apartment."

Walker pulled out a slip of paper from his pocket. He read it again, frowned, and tossed it across the table. Jack took it. "What's this?"

"Leslie's phone number. She gave it to me. Look at the sevens, Jack."

Jack looked down and handed it back. "Looks like the lab was right."

The dessert now tasted vile. "Now, what do I do?"

"Nothing. Play her and see what she discloses to you."

"Romance her, is that it, Jack?"

"Until we understand the connection between her and Whittaker, or find him first."

Walker said, "Maybe they fooled around, and that's it. Maybe it's nothing."

"I don't care about sex, unless it explains his disappearance, and there's one more thing. I found out that the Russians might've had a lever on Whittaker. Gambling debts."

Jack took out the Russian coin. Walker asked what it was, and Jack explained to Walker how he had obtained the coin from Sheldon and his conversation with the Russian in the Soviet sector.

"Leslie, Whittaker, and now, Russians?"

Jack returned to his xerograph. "Look at the numbers there, and then at what she gave you."

"What am I supposed to see now?"

"Look at the ones. Americans don't make their ones or sevens like that."

Walker looked at her numeral 1. With a small upright harpoon, it looked as if it hung on the page. Her 7 had a rigid top bar that descended into a curve with a slash through it. Walker looked to Jack. "And this proves what?"

"It's possible Leslie is British. Some training on the accent and we would never know."

"You read her file from Davies, Jack."

"I read what was I meant to see."

"Are you saying Davies is part of the con?"

"Or he was conned." Jack nudged the coin in front of Walker. "Return this coin to Sheldon for me and ask him where the underground types with money in Vienna meet."

"Meet for what?" Walker tried to keep the tone of his voice neutral.

"Black-market goods. Whatever makes money."

Jack asked about his last interaction with Leslie. Walker summarized their two dates, from the night of schnapps and wine, down to the dishes and drinks ordered at the bistro. He left out the bit about her asking him up to her place, and the cat.

Jack asked, "Think you made an impression on her?"

"I have no idea. We went out twice, so that's something."

"Or she wanted a second drink of water at the well."

"Thanks for the boost that's a kick in the pants, Jack. You said play her. Any advice?"

"Act aloof. It'll make her think she's misread you, which will make her anxious."

"Anxious?"

"Nothing is more devastating to a woman than a loss of confidence."

"You give me too much credit, Jack, and I'm not convinced you're an expert on women. You assume she cares about me."

"Whether she cares about you or not, doesn't matter. This is about her ego."

"Thanks for another compliment."

"I'm sorry to be so harsh, Walker. This has nothing to do with gender. Jack's finger tapped the table to emphasize his next point. "In this game we play, everything is a lie."

"Everything?" Walker asked.

Jack leaned forward, eyes intent. "Here's the thing that separates us from civilians. Everything, including the story we tell ourselves to get to sleep at night, or to get through the day, is a lie. We know it, but civilians don't. They have lost track of all the lies because they are too busy reacting to everything around them. They have neither the time nor the energy to think and analyze what is before them, only to react."

"And we're different because we keep track of the lies?"

Jack shook his head. "No, the difference is we have a mission, and we must never lose sight of it. Each person has a job, and it's when someone strays from their role that everything becomes complicated and potentially compromised. Everything is fouled up beyond all repair."

"Beyond all repair?" Walker smiled. "We used to say FUBAR, but in time we'll say snafu."

"We adapt, Walker, because that's what we do. Every mission has contingency plans and countermeasures. Trust the mission, Walker."

"And did your plan include Meeks?"

"Let me worry about Meeks." Jack reached for the newspaper. "Karlsruhe called. This assassination has them worried." Jack rose from the table. He folded the paper such that the lead article was visible.

Knowing that the Viennese custom was to leave the paper for the next customer, Walker asked, "What's with taking the paper?"

Jack winked. "I thought our British friends across the room might enjoy it. Stay, finish your chocolate there, and watch them. I'll take care of the bill on my way out."

Jack approached a table with two Cambridge types on surveillance detail. Jack placed the paper on their table. He leaned over, and said to them both, "Damn shame, all the violence in this world."

Chapter Eighteen

He knocked twice, convinced the man inside had heard him. Walker was about to knock again, with more intent, when the bolt turned and the door opened.

He started to say something but didn't because he saw the unexpected, a young girl. Green eyes, arrogant cheekbones, her hair long and combed over in a part that sent a platinum wave over a shoulder, she stared at him. He kept his surprise behind his eyes. Sheldon appeared. "Walker?"

"May I come in?"

Sheldon widened the door, but the girl stood there like some ethereal sentinel.

Breakfast was in the air—the sizzle of eggs and the scent of strong coffee.

"May I take your coat?"

Walker surrendered it and Sheldon directed him to the table.

"Like some breakfast?"

The girl placed a dish of eggs with a generous side of hashed potatoes topped with a dash of paprika in front him. She left and returned with a cup of coffee. He saw no choice but to pick up the fork and sample hospitality. Two orange eyes of egg yolks stared up at him from the dish. "I wasn't expecting this," he said.

"And I wasn't expecting you," Sheldon replied. The girl sat opposite Walker with her own coffee and eggs. She looked Sheldon's way for what Walker interpreted as permission to eat her breakfast. His yolks bled out into the hash.

Walker placed the coin on the table. "Jack asked me to return this to you.

He met the good Russian in the bad part of town."

"Good and bad. You think the world is that simple."

"I know it's not, and no philosophy with breakfast, please. It's too early. I'm looking for information, and I wondered if you can help me."

"I helped Jack, and now I help you, is that it?"

"The Russian told Jack that Whittaker might be involved with gamblers." The girl sat there, her eyes back and forth, as she watched the tennis match. "I'm not a guide dog, Walker."

"But you do know where gamblers meet, don't you?"

"Why should I help you?"

Walker looked at the girl then at Sheldon. "Maybe I can help you with her?"

Sheldon's face twitched. "What do you mean 'help'?"

"Maybe Jack and I can get her out of Vienna, to wherever her family is."

"She has no family."

"That makes it easier. Pick a destination, and we'll see what we can do."

Sheldon put his hand on the back of the girl's shoulders. Walker watched the hand disappear under the long cascade of blonde hair. He said something into her ear and she left the room. He waited until she disappeared. "How do I know I can trust you?"

"Same way I know I can trust you."

"She needs to be safe. She's a child."

"Something tells me she can take care of herself."

"She's an innocent, Walker."

"I believe that like I believe dentistry is pain-free."

"These Russians, they can be found at night in the Simmering district."

Walker reviewed the highlights of his mental reel. The district was home to museums. "That's the 11th district and British territory. Anywhere specific?"

"Zentralfriedhof."

"The cemetery?"

"It's perfect for illegal exchanges and meetings."

"Which part of the marble orchard?" Walker asked.

"Soviet section, of course."

"Of course, but can you narrow it down for me since it's huge?"

The cemetery was the largest graveyard in Europe. Sheldon scratched the side of his head. "There are several good locations. There's the crematorium near the Friedhof der Namenlosen, and then there are any one of the four gasometers."

Walker took a chance. "Something else came up that I'd like to run pass you. The British have gone all nelly over a recent assassination. You might want to put in your hat to expect an unusual display of British manners around town." Walker glanced to the newspaper on the table. Sheldon said that he had read an article on the dead Swede. "Do you have an opinion on the matter?"

"Some topics are best not discussed amongst friends."

"Or allies," Walker said. "I can see why you're in no hurry for Israel."

"Your take on the event?"

"Terrorists, why?"

"Today's terrorists are tomorrow's heroes and politicians."

Walker swam past it. "I need to find Whittaker."

"If he's with the Russians, he has made his choice, so I have to ask why?"

"I don't have time to explain why," Walker said.

"This isn't a game of cowboys and Indians, Walker. You have to remember that here, most people hope the Indians win."

The girl came back into the room, stood there, and Walker was unsure whether she'd been listening, or how much she understood because she remained silent. Sheldon held up the coin for Walker to see. "Do you know the German word for 'debt'?"

"Die Pflicht?"

"Die Schuld is the better word."

Walker blinked. "Isn't that the word for guilt?"

"Precisely."

Chapter Nineteen

It was late, an afternoon at the office. He'd seen Leslie give him the eye several times. When he approached her, she walked away. He was in no mood to repeat high school, the drama of a bad date or breakup. If he closed his door, she would have to barge in on some pretense or other, but he decided to leave the door open.

Now and then she walked past his office. Her profile in a dress didn't help him any. Not that guilt gnawed at him, but he had that feeling a guy had when he shouldn't have kissed a girl, but had, and she wanted to know his intentions.

After his café meeting with Jack, Walker tried to figure out how best to follow Jack's directive to play Leslie. He was no actor, and he'd been promoted from understudy to lead in the play. This was a big role, his debut, and he was unprepared.

And then there was what Jack had said about her nationality. British.

She tapped the doorframe and said hello. She could say it a thousand times and he would never have believed she was a mole. Somewhere between her smile and whatever excuse she had for visiting him, their eyes met. She leaned forward to pick up something from his blotter. She presented her cleavage. He hated himself for the stolen look. She smirked when she caught him as if to let him know that she didn't mind the theft.

"I was beginning to think that you were ignoring me."

She sat in the chair in front of him, uninvited. He was grateful he couldn't see her legs.

"It's impossible to ignore you, Leslie. I've been preoccupied."

"The ribbons?" she asked.

"That and Whittaker missing, and Meeks."

"Since we can't use typewriters, how are we to do our notes?"

He tapped the side of his head with his forefinger, "All of it goes in here for now."

He found it curious that she didn't respond to the names Whittaker and Meeks.

"Good a place as any, I guess."

She smiled, and he wanted to kiss her. She had to know it. She squirmed in her chair the way a cat settled in for a long and comfortable stay. "I was wondering if you had any plans to visit me again," she said. "I enjoyed my time with you, and I'd like to think you enjoyed yourself. You know, I could make dinner at my place, unless you prefer to go out."

"I'm worried that I might fail the final exam in algebra."

"What if I promise no talk about maths. Interested, dinner at my place, tomorrow night, unless you have other plans?"

She wrinkled her eyes in a way that suggested mischief, but he didn't arch an eyebrow at her slip. She had said 'maths,' a British term for mathematics.

He told her the truth. "The only thing I've been doing at night is trying to find Whittaker. Tomorrow night sounds good."

She repeated her address. Walker found to his surprise that he wouldn't have to initiate Jack's directive to engage her. She made it easier for him. She had come to him.

"Find your way to my place by 1800?"

"I can and I will. Six o'clock it is."

She stood up and he watched her, aware that she knew his eyes were on her. She stopped and turned as if to catch the naughty schoolboy "Oh," she said, "I hope I don't have to compete with Betty Grable."

Chapter Twenty

The hunt for Whittaker had yielded no fruit for Walker. Every café worth going to, worth being seen in, he visited. He had ambled past the Hotel Imperial enough times for the doorman to tip his hat at him. He had lost enough money at backgammon, card games, and chess in bars and dives to make his face known as a loser, with a capital L. Nobody nibbled at rumor, innuendo, or showed an interest in the existence of a man with a Constantine coin.

He doled out all the right whispers to the wrong people. Nothing. He had insinuated that he was a man with money, hot with information, and all of that drew him nothing but dull stares, occasional shrugs, and the too-frequent walk-away. Every strategy led him nowhere.

He tried to make himself an easy mark. He sat in the back of the bar as the hopeless lush romantic, but that charade failed, too. He pretended to down lots of vodka or gin, when it was cold water substituted for alcohol.

Nothing. Nichts.

Women came and went. They huddled around him, brushed his hair off his forehead, offered him drinks and themselves. Two ladies once argued over who should take him home before deciding that they both would share him. Tempted, he declined.

Then there were men. Some were working-class types who offered a slap of solace on the shoulder or nodded in agreement over woes and then tilted back the drinks he bought them. Other men, the ones who wore perfume, offered to take him home. Some moved in too close, but he enjoyed their company, the conversations, though they left him unsettled.

Walker decided to visit the bone yard, to look for the living among the dead. He entered the Zentralfriedhof from Tor 9, one of the numerous gates into the cemetery.

Under a crepuscular sky, all the markers and graves were white teeth among the weeds. He saw the ornate mausoleums, the cupola of the anti-Semite Karl Lueger, the city mayor, in the distance. He walked through a small sea of black crosses for the Wehrmacht dead, and he viewed the memorial to the Russian dead in the Great War. He looked up at the statues of two Red Army soldiers. Their flags of stone tipped down to the earth. It would've all played cinematic, exalted and tragic, and morbid had it not been for the unexpected pheasants among the gravestones.

Only the dead slept here.

Walker realized he was standing among the graves of honor, the Ehrengräber. He saw the gilded bee and his heart sank. In front of him stood the stone obelisk, and a gold bee hovered on high, caught forever in flight inside a circle.

Here lay his nemesis Beethoven.

Walker wanted to hate the man, but he couldn't. He thought of Peggy.

Sonata quasi una fantasia, or 'sonata sort of like a fantasy' haunted him.

He had lost Peggy to it.

Opus 27, Number 2, movement one, adagio sostenuto. He looked at the composer's tomb. It had more flowers than Mozart's memorial on the left. Walker asked Wolfgang how he felt about Ludwig having plagiarized his *Don Giovanni*. No answer. He imagined Mozart's laughs, the composer telling him that the original idea for the Commendatore's death scene came to him while he was having his way with Constanze in triplet meter. Walker didn't bother looking for the memorial to Franz Schubert. His eyes returned to the stone monument.

He remembered everything.

Peggy had taken piano lessons from a traveling Romeo who had made every girl in town sigh. The man was handsome, had nice hands. He represented culture where farms and rows of corn reigned. Walker admitted his jealousy and insecurity to her. Peggy ministered assurances that he, Walker, was the one she loved. He remembered all of it while he read the letter that lived in infamy for his heart.

Seeing her penmanship, and hoping for a minute trace of her perfume on the pages, knowing that she had held that piece of paper in her hands was what had gotten him through the hells that he knew he never would forget for the rest of his life. He glossed over the musical terminology because he didn't know Italian. She wrote about Herr Beethoven and her adulation for her piano teacher. Walker's idea of moonlight in *Moonlight Sonata* was reconnaissance, and avoiding snipers, hidden in the belfry of churches.

Then the day had come. He had received his Dear John letter on 13th December, 1944, the day he and his men had been relieved at the Colmar Pocket. Covered in blood and cold to the bone, he cried after he read it.

She said that she had to be honest, that she loved him too much to hide anything from him. She said that she couldn't forgive herself and that she understood if he never forgave her. She said she didn't know what had come over her, but Walker knew what had happened. He didn't blame her. He blamed *him*.

Her teacher had suggested one day that she come to his place so he could play the *Sonata of the Woods* for her alone on his pianoforte, because, as he had said, the first movement is too delicate to play on a modern piano. She had gone innocently enough. He had told her that it was a special reward for all her hard work.

The scenario played out in his mind. The Lothario keyed the melancholic movement, as Beethoven had instructed 'without the dampers,' which meant for him holding more than the sustain pedal down in his simulation of the artist summoning the immortals. He played the music as Beethoven would have, as an attack without any pause in the enchantment.

All Walker's numb brain could think of as he read the stained letter was his own masochistic image of Peggy reclining nude, arms back, breasts balanced on the man's piano bench, his Helen of Troy abducted in the piano teacher's private Montparnasse.

That was December 1944, when Walker received his second Bronze Star and his first broken heart.

Chapter Twenty-One

The clock on the wall the next morning said 0900. Walker spread his feet under the desk, his face no happier than day-old lettuce, but he did think about his date with Leslie later.

Jack couldn't decide whether to sneeze or not. Walker looked to him. The sneeze never came. Jack tapped his briefcase next to his chair to check that it was still there.

They waited.

They looked at the clock again.

They stared at the mahogany table that was waxed with such unerring devotion that the buildup would entrap a fingerprint for all eternity. Jack took out a pfennig and flicked it across the table's surface with his index finger. They both watched it sail across the wood before it fell off the other side.

The door handle turned. Meeks and Major General Davies entered the room.

Davies was the first to speak. "Morning, gentlemen."

Behind Meeks was his silver tea set in Leslie's hands. There was a fat breakfast pastry on a lace doily. She placed the service on the table without looking up. Davies started the meeting after Leslie left. "Mr. Meeks says there have been developments. He will ask for a status on Whittaker later."

Their eyes watched Meeks. A stir and light clink, then a tap of the spoon, then the man spoke. "I was perplexed last time we met about this matter with Whittaker, and this office's slow pace in the recruitment of former Nazi personnel. In light of recent intelligence, I've become more concerned and curious as to why Jack Marshall would meet with a Soviet operative."

Jack checked himself. "You had me followed?"

"So you don't deny it?" Meeks tore apart a croissant with his fingers.

Jack gave Meeks a look that did all the work of a knife. "Why would I deny meeting a potential source?"

"We are on the same side, Mr. Marshall."

"I wonder, Mr. Meeks. You had me watched, but who watches you?"

Davies tried distraction. "We have important business to discuss."

Meeks reached for some papers. "Walker, when we last met I gave Jack a list, and I presume he gave you the assignment."

"Yes, sir, he did."

Meeks selected a pen. "And do you have a status on any of the names?" Meeks lifted a sheet of paper from his stack that Walker assumed was a copy of the one given to Jack. Meeks read off the first name.

Walker gave a synopsis of the man's past, a history of his war-time conduct, some data as to possible collusion in war crimes, and finally, a verdict on the man's value to the Company. Walker's short sentences diagrammed his assessments, rationales, and conclusions.

An hour ticked away, during which Jack and Major General Davies listened to Walker without interruption. The only sound in the room was Meeks making furious notes. Jack glanced to the General, who smiled before he replaced it with his serious business face. Walker was doing well, and Jack was proud.

Walker stopped. Meeks kept taking notes for a moment then ceased writing. He rested his pen on the table and pinched the top of his nose. "I must say, Walker, that I'm impressed with the amount of detail in your report. I now understand why Mr. Marshall selected you for this job, but I must admit that I'm a little confused."

"Confused about what, sir?"

"How is that you remember places, dates, times, people, and you don't have a shred of paper in front of you for a reference?"

"I have a good memory, sir."

Meeks used his pen to tap his notes. It was a dramatic gesture. Pure theatre.

"Without any corroboration, it's meaningless."

"Corroboration, sir?" Walker said.

"I simply can't take your word for all of this." He dropped his pen on top of his papers.

Jack's voice, soft though it was, cut through the man's dismissal. "There is corroboration for everything that he said, Mr. Meeks."

"Really?" Meeks' voice intimated surprise. His mouth tightened at the corners, the eyes sharpened with suspicion. "Care to elaborate?"

Jack looked to his side, down at the floor. Jack's hand reached for his briefcase there, out of view to Meeks. With some effort, Jack hoisted up a thick folder. He opened it, and pages crinkled from the handwriting and the weight of important facts. Meeks and Davies watched, as Jack turned a page or two in search of a location. Jack didn't look up.

"Here it is," he said. "My notes after each one of Walker's interviews." Jack rattled off names. He repeated dates, time, and locations. He selected and read excerpts that supported Walker's statements.

"An interviewee mentioned Auer Company. Army intelligence corroborated that the scientists at Auer worked with uranium." Jack ruffled some more pages, back and forth. "There are uranium mines in Czechoslovakia and in Asia, and by Asia, I mean Russia."

More movement. More stiff pages.

"German scientists Walker had mentioned had worked on nickel barriers, and another group was into isotope separation, and some mumbo-jumbo called heavy water. All Greek to me, but I have it all in excruciating detail here." Jack's finger tapped a page. "I have nine and twelve-digit numbers, probably code, which must mean God knows what, but then these five-digit numbers that I'm looking at remind me of transport numbers we used in the army. My guess is that somebody is playing mailman between the Germans and the Russians, with the Post Office somewhere in Eastern Europe."

Jack closed the folder and rested it against his chest. He stared at Meeks.

Meeks motioned with his hand. He asked for the folder.

"No."

Meeks looked as if someone had broken all the eggs in his delivery from the corner store. "What do you mean, no?"

"I mean, 'No,' I won't give you my papers. See, the way I look at it, Mr. Meeks, is that while the Germans are selling their goods and secrets to us, I don't feel comfortable with whatever stake the British might have in this matter, and you are as British as the Union Jack."

"Dammit, Jack," Davies said. They're our allies. Meeks is one of us."

"Is he?"

Meeks stiffened in his chair. "Might I remind you that I am a member of the Oversight Committee, and your actions here are tantamount to contempt in a court of law. I could have you subpoenaed."

"Do that, Mr. Meeks. I'd welcome the opportunity to speak before a tribunal."

Davies whispered, "Jack, I hope you know what you're doing."

"I hope so, too, General. See, Mr. Meeks has to trot himself and his tea set all the way back to the States. He'll have to wake up some judge in the middle of the night and recite his spiel to get his subpoena, then find his way back to Vienna to have it served."

Meeks turned red. "Why would I have to do that when I can make a phone call to Berlin? We have military judges there who would be happy to execute the writ."

Jack smiled. "Insubordination is even better than contempt of court. I know most of the judges in Berlin. Justices Biddle and Parker would be happy to sit and listen all Solomon-like to what you and I have to say about each other. You may know them from the Nuremberg Trials."

Meeks slammed his fist against the table. "Why must you be so difficult?"

"And why do you stay at the Hotel Sacher?" Jack deposited his folder into his briefcase. Everyone heard the metal click snap. Jack's eyes returned to Meeks. "Have an answer as to why the Sacher?"

"What difference does it make where I stay?"

"All the difference, Meeks," Jack dropped the pretense of the salutation Mister. "I find it peculiar that after your precious silver tea set made its debut my office was burgled. All of my typewriter ribbons are MIA. Of course, nobody ever thought that I kept notes. And you want me to hand over everything. I don't think so." Jack paused. "Tell me, Meeks, are your friends at the Hotel Sacher from Oxford or Cambridge?"

"That's enough, Jack," Davies said.

"No, General, it's not. If I had my way, I'd subpoena Meeks to find out what's what, between him and the British."

Davies was standing now. "What are you implying?"

"How do we know our allies aren't working against us?"

"You're mad," Meeks said.

Jack smiled. "Don't you mean, 'you're nuts'?"

Davies pointed a finger at Jack, "Think twice, Jack, and make life easier for all of us and hand those damn notes over to Meeks. I'd rather fight the Germans again before I fight some bureaucracy with pocket-protectors for experience. Politics back home have gone nasty, and I don't think you've got the stomach for it, Jack. I know I don't."

"Listen to the general," Meeks said.

Davies pivoted and directed his ire at Meeks. "You don't get off that easy. If I find out you are shorting us, I'll throw you out of the plane on the way back to the States myself. Quote me, and stick that in your notes to the Oversight Committee."

Meeks corkscrewed in his seat, agitated, like a washer machine. "Mr. Marshall says that after my visit, his office was broken into."

"What of it?" Davies said.

"Has anyone thought to consider the Jew?"

Davies glared at Meeks. "Are you serious?"

"The man is killing Nazis."

Davis seemed at a loss for words until he wasn't. "There's no evidence, and if he were I couldn't give a damn. Most of them deserve it. Hell, some of the ones we're hiding deserve to walk the thirteen steps up to a noose and a trapdoor. All I care about is that he doesn't kill anyone before we interview them."

"And that he has done, General. Forget the doctor at the asylum?"

"Blame the Jew, is that your answer, Meeks?" Davis said.

"Until you give me a better suspect."

Davies fumed. "There are times when I think all of this would've been avoided had FDR listened to the State Department's reports that Hitler planned to exterminate European Jewry. No, the president ignored the reconnaissance photographs of the camps. If the man had listened, none of us would be here."

"You don't know that," Meeks said. "I'm well aware of the meeting, and the one the president had with Rabbi Wise and his delegation. The fact is this is not 1942; it's 1948, and we are in Vienna. The man is a suspect in several assassinations, and he looks good for the stolen typewriter ribbons."

"Unless you have any evidence he pinched those ribbons, I suggest you tend to your small garden here for your committee, and stay the hell out of my way."

"Or what, General? I am the lead. I am the head of the committee here, and the future existence of the Company depends on my report."

"We'll see about that." Davies about spat his sentence out and stormed out.

Meeks gathered up his belongings like a petulant teenager. Both Jack and Walker watched him. Meeks left with a loud slam of the door behind him.

Walker and Jack sat there. A housefly landed on the table. Both of them watched it. The fly walked, stopped, walked some more before it rubbed its thin legs, tasting the wax on the table.

"About those notes?" Walker said.

"The Nazis weren't the only ones who learned not to leave a paper trial."

The metal clasp unclicked. The file folder slid across the glossy surface to Walker. The insect flew off. Walker looked down. He flipped through several pages, while Jack talked.

"Most of the pages are blank," he said. "On some of them I scribbled nonsense, and on others, I cut and pasted newspaper pictures and articles to beef up the visual from a distance. It also makes the pages seem old and noisy."

"And that bit about the Auer Company? Where did that come from?"

"Intelligence briefs I've read. Nothing new."

"What do you think Meeks will make of it all?"

"If Meeks is behind the theft of the ribbons, he'll push hard for this folder, because he'll think that he and his British friends are out in the cold."

"And the threat of a subpoena?"

"He'll want to see what the folder says before it is aired out in front of any committee."

They watched the fly land on the slippery surface. The insect wheeled like a plane and his eyes faced them, seeing in all directions except from above.

Their chairs moved.

The fly disappeared.

Chapter Twenty-Two

Sheldon slept. Memory moved along muscle and his breathing made sharp stabbing sounds. He dreamt of white hands that grabbed him. Inhuman noises assaulted his ears and a foul stench crawled up his nose and invaded his brain. He heard voices, panic in them, and gasps. He watched naked bodies fall down like marionettes, their heads forward.

That was how he found them when he was sent in to collect and remove the dead. He moved through a harvest of flesh, from one end of the room to the other. He lifted corpses onto the wheelbarrow. Now and then there would be a body too heavy for him, so he whistled for assistance and another sonderkommando would take the feet, he, the hands, and they swung the cargo into the transport. Hour after hour of this, so his days went. He'd seen all manner of faces. Some of the gassed were at peace, others contorted. He'd find a friend, see an acquaintance. The endless cargo moved into one end of the brick house and came out as ashes for the pits near the birch trees at the other end. Flames ate the flesh fed to them.

He tossed, turned, and came to rest on his back. They pull at his gray uniform, mock him, push him one way so he turned another way. They call him 'muser,' Yiddish for traitor. They throw their own ashes on him. He started to choke and lose his way through the mist of gray and white. As he made his way out of the womb of death, one of the creatures seized hold of him. Up close he looked into empty eye sockets, saw the faded hair that clung to the skull, as blue lips mouthed words without a voice.

Then he saw her among the imperishable shadows.

His arm pawed at the air to get to her but she avoided him. It was his mother.

He tried to tell her that he had not abandoned her. That he loved her but she can't hear him. She swept a kerchief over her head, as he had seen her do a thousand times as a child, when she was leaving the house. He shoved others away to get to her, to get near her. His mother raised a hand and said something to him in Russian. Then she disappeared.

"Sheldon, Sheldon, wake up."

It was Tania.

His mother had told him in Russian, "Be a witness." She had used the imperative. He remembered that tone to her voice when he was a little boy, when his silliness tested her patience. The sharp edge to her voice would freeze him into obedience.

Tania's grip had forced his eyes open. He could feel the air from the open window. The moonlight was pulled into the room and into Tania's blonde hair.

He wanted to cry.

"Close your eyes and go to sleep," she said. "No more bad dreams tonight."

He closed his eyes but opened them again. Her hand comforted him.

"You can sleep now. I will keep you safe."

Chapter Twenty-Three

Walker purchased a pastry mélange and had it boxed up for his date with Leslie. He'd bought wine from a merchant. His colloquial German was improving. His performance of the evening, however, would be in English and at Leslie's apartment.

Walker had managed to get beyond the double glass doors in the lobby this time, climb those Kilimanjaro stairs of hers to her door. A sober knock, and Leslie answered the door. She had a talent for décor. He had no idea what the original apartment looked like, but her touch was evident throughout the apartment. The walls were blue, and white blinds hung from the windows. A sisal rug covered a section of hardwood floors. Thonet and Eames for chairs. Leslie was a modular modern woman.

Walker didn't know what would be on the menu, either for food or conversation, especially now that he was in her territory. Everything played like a movie at the theatre, with himself as the heckler in the back row. She let him in. She accepted the small box of pastries and the bottle of wine from him. She insisted that he take his jacket off. He hung it up in the closet along with Grable. He liked her place. He confessed that he knew nothing about wine, joked that there ought to be a nursery rhyme that could teach men how to pair wine with food.

"Cocktail before dinner?" she asked.

"Scotch on the rocks if you have it," he answered.

He realized that this was his first home-cooked meal since he arrived in Vienna. Something smelled good and delicious and the scent emanated from the kitchen. The score to this movie moved along at a nice, gay pace. No shrieking violins from a horror show played.

Leslie returned from her kitchen with two small Baccarat glasses. Crystal was a theme with her. It gave Walker hopes for clarity. "Shall we?"

Whatever brand she poured made the ice cube crack and shudder, a sound safe on land but not at sea. She handed him his drink and he said, "I thought most women preferred champagne."

The Scotch burned his tongue as retribution for his naive opener.

"And what made you think I'm most women?"

He noticed the swank Probber daybed behind her. He complimented her on the interior design. His quarters, by crude comparison, were Spartan, functional, simple.

"Dinner will be ready in a bit," she said.

"What are we having?"

"A simple roast with vegetables. Nothing fancy. I hope you'll enjoy it." She pulled a chain for the tall lamp on a spindle near him. The metallic sound elicited a nervous tic. "Do sudden sounds make you nervous?" she asked.

"A relic from the war," he answered.

Act, act, act. He felt his cue coming. Drink in hand, she rested her forearms Sphinx-like on the cushion's edge. "Do I make you nervous?" she asked. "I'm sorry, that was uncalled for."

"It's okay, you can't help yourself."

Her voice was cautious but curious. "What does that mean?"

"Always analyzing. The job."

"I see. You think I'm some cold fish."

"It came out wrong," he said. "I am algebra, and you're calculus. We've covered this."

"Algebra might've been unfair." She had bent her elbow and rested the side of her face against her hand. "You're agile and know how to adapt to difficult situations. You're intelligent. Loyal. Self-effacing but wounded."

"Wounded?" Walker held his drink.

"Why didn't you go back home and become another Joe?"

The question felt savage. "According to you, it's because I can't think for myself."

"This is your chance to set the record straight," she said and offered a smile.

"Home wasn't an option. My mother had passed."

"I'm sorry to hear that," she said.

"There were relatives but they had their own lives to live."

"And Jack called with a proposition?"

"Something like that."

She listened, expressionless.

"Jack has always been honest with me. He said it was an important job, that he couldn't explain too much, but he thought I was a good fit. He said I would like it."

"As time went on, did you?"

"Like the job?"

She nodded.

"Then or now?"

"You tell me." And with that she picked up her drink and took a tiny sip to wet her lips. He guessed Torquemada used to get thirsty, too. He decided to initiate his own interrogation.

"And how did you come into your line of work?"

She shrugged. "I knew languages, which is a rare commodity, regardless of sex. It's a skill that attracts the agencies. Before they acknowledged my talent, I was a Girl Friday who typed up reports. I pointed out things that others missed. Superiors noticed, and from there my responsibilities and involvement increased. At some point, Davies became aware of me, and the rest is history, as they say."

Leslie knew what to say because it flowed like water over or under ice.

"What kind of things did you point out?" he asked.

"Discrepancies, or I'd make suggestions to improve operations."

"Like some kind of office Mata Hari?"

"She got caught and was executed. I wasn't," she said it with some mischief. "You said Jack trusted you?"

"Did I?"

She didn't smile. "Do you trust Jack?"

"Why wouldn't I?" She listened. He said, "We have history. Do you trust

Davies?"

"Trust him with what? Davies became my superior and there are orders."

A timer dinged in the kitchen to end the round. He rose and offered to help. She declined his assistance and moved into the kitchen. He heard the oven door open and the shrill pull of the rack. She asked that he open the wine. Walker realized he needed a corkscrew. She must've anticipated his need because she tossed it to him. She turned her attention to the rump roast.

As he wormed the cork up from the bottle, she set down a dish full of roasted vegetables, and when the cork popped she stood before him with a carving knife. He poured the wine for her to taste. She said she liked it, so he poured more into her glass and some into his.

"Was your mother a good cook?" she asked.

"She was, and I'm confident that she would've liked this roast from the look of it to ask you for the recipe."

*　*　*

After their meal, Leslie found an ashtray, another Baccarat piece. The crystal had enough heft to it to double as a shot put. He offered her a cigarette. She said no. He waited a few minutes before he asked her another question. It had begun to rain. It was a soft, lazy patter against the windowpane.

"You look as if you have something on your mind," she said.

"I'm curious. It takes more than languages and analysis to be successful at what we do."

She smiled and responded, "Are we talking about physical abilities?"

"There comes a point, where, you know, you have to be able to handle yourself."

She shifted one leg under the other. "You're right, but you've forgotten two things, Walker."

"Have I?"

"We're in the business of cultivating relationships."

"And the second thing?"

"As a rule, men underestimate women, meaning they don't see us as a physical threat."

"What about you?" Walker asked her.

"What about me?"

"You could've returned to civilian life." She didn't answer so he inquired further. "Any family? No nice boy from Shaker Heights waiting for you?" Leslie seemed to twitch either at the suggestion of a man in her life or at the name, Shaker Heights. Walker went in for the close-up now. "Should I not pry?"

"There was no man in the picture." The wine had made her lips crimson and attractive. "As for family, I'm my mother's disappointment with no marriage or prospects."

The rain fell with a tight rhythm outside.

"You said I was agile and I adapt well to situations."

She eyed him. "You have a good memory."

"No brighter than the next Joe or Harry out there. I learned how to survive."

She cradled her wineglass in one hand. "And what about those wounds?"

"I was bayoneted in a forest once." Walker toyed with his cigarette, waiting for the best time to light it for dramatic effect. "I've had some other scratches along the way, but none worth mentioning."

She took another sip of wine, eyes on him. "I was thinking about Peggy. Is she not a wound, too?"

He hadn't expected that. He thought back to her with the carving knife. Her question about Peggy was the blade in and out of him without a trace of blood. "Does analysis require that you test pulse points and scars?"

"It's a reflex, and I shouldn't have."

An apology would've been an admission, a sign of weakness. He was going in. "What about you and Whittaker?" She sipped, said nothing. "Anything between you two?"

"Only sex."

"You're candid. I like that."

"Do you? Like that, I mean. You're not a prude, thank God."

"I do like a little to the imagination. You?"

"I know what I like, and I'm not afraid to go after it."

He pulled the proverbial trigger. "And that includes Whittaker?"

"I've had to contend with Victorian sensibilities all my life, Walker. I came from a modest family, struggled to get an education, since my brothers came first. I've served my country with distinction and then what? Without a man, I'm left with few choices for a job to support myself, and then there's every woman's curse."

"What curse?" he asked.

"The unforgiveable sin of growing old." He sensed both anger and sorrow in her voice, but she added another observation before he could respond. She said, "People in the office think I'm a secretary, and I resent it."

"You're more than a secretary, Leslie, and you know it."

"The women at work seem to think I did something sexual to have my own office."

"No casting couch there. You served your country with distinction, like you said."

"They don't know that, and what's with the questions about Whittaker?"

"The man is missing."

She seem disappointed with his answer. "No interest in salacious details then?"

"It's none of my business. I couldn't care less if the two of you played chess, Tarzan and Jane, or read Byron to each other. I don't care."

"Good to know you're not the jealous type."

"Peggy taught me that people will do whatever they want, regardless of what you think and feel."

"She really hurt you, didn't she?" Leslie sat on the edge of the loveseat. "Whittaker and I were long over before he disappeared, before you showed up in Vienna. It's not relevant."

"That's not for you to decide, especially with Meeks around."

She looked at him hard. He had seen concrete walls that were softer.

"And what about you and Peggy?" she asked.

The question came out of left field, and he had to return the ball with an answer.

CHAPTER TWENTY-THREE

"Like Whittaker, she's ancient history."

"You don't get it, do you, Walker?"

"Apparently, I don't." He realized that he had never lit his cigarette, but he remembered that it was raining outside. It would be a miserable trek back to his place. He started to get up.

"Where are you going?" she asked, startled. "We still have dessert."

He looked at her. The look said that he wanted her to dig a grave and that he hoped that she would jump into it after the foul ball of mentioning Peggy again. He ambled over to the closet. He found Grable.

He heard her say it. "I don't think Whittaker is coming back."

Walker straightened out his sleeves under his jacket. "Is that feminine intuition or mathematical analysis?"

Her eyes narrowed. "I don't know, and that's the truth."

"Truth is a commodity in Vienna." He lit his cigarette, which meant that he would have to sit down and use the ashtray. "Play straight with me, and we'll see what we can make of this mess."

"So like a man that he thinks he can fix every problem," she said.

"That's not what I meant, so don't put words in my mouth. I asked you to play straight with me, so let's be adults about this. You admitted to sex with Whittaker, so what's there to be shy about? Talk to me."

"Whittaker got himself mixed up with some Russians. He was looking to make fast money so he could knock off when he returned to the States. Take it easy, you know."

"The worst kind of money is the easy kind. What was the score?" he asked.

"A rare coin."

"Anything else?"

"He did a few small things for the Russians to gain their confidence. Nothing major."

"What kind of things?" He studied her. Her movements seemed honest.

"Rough up a few lads, anything he thought that might get him closer to the coin."

"Did the tough stuff include Nazis?"

She nodded.

"A certain gentleman found in a loony bin?"

That she didn't answer was an answer.

"I see. And what do you know about that gentleman in the nuthouse?"

Leslie looked to the bottle of wine. He said, "Have more of your drink if you want."

She poured herself a splash. "Whittaker didn't know the man was on Jack's list. He didn't have a name or description. He thought that when he knocked the man around, it'd put him in good with the Russians and a thrashing would shake some information loose, info they wanted."

"And what were they looking for?" he asked.

"Collectibles, rarities and other treasures, but then it all went wrong."

"Usually does." Walker put the cigarette in his mouth. "And then what?"

"He brought the man here."

"Here? That's a stupid move, now the Russians know where you live."

"And I'm a witness," she said. "Whittaker never did think things through."

Walker agreed. "I'll say."

She knew her man. Whittaker moved through life as if his shoelaces were tied together. She pointed to one of the Thonet chairs. "He sat over there. Whittaker asked about the coin, but the man babbled on about uranium, and something about postal boxes."

"Postal boxes?"

"He repeated 'Post Box 1037P' over and over again."

"Anything else?"

"Something about codes from Molotov to Moscow, and I.G. Farben."

"And what did Whittaker do when the spigot gave him more than water?"

"Whittaker hit him to shut him up."

"Enough to kill him?"

"No."

"Lucky him, and these Russians, they moved the Q and A elsewhere?"

"Yes, but it wasn't just Russians who took him," she said.

"Who then?"

"British."

"Their accents gave them away?" Walker asked.

"It was the way they were dressed. One of them had his hair slicked back in a Boston. He wore a long coat, a waistcoat, thin tie, a Mr. B collar, and his trousers were high. Oh, and brothel creepers for shoes."

"Quite the visual, and excellent recall, Leslie. Anything else before they split?"

"They said the Nazi was theirs. Oh, and I almost forgot. One of these men had a bag with him. He put it on the floor. I remember now because my cat nosed around the bag. He became upset about the cat near the bag, so he threw the cat out the door."

"What happened next?"

"The two Brits took the Nazi and Whittaker, and stormed out of here."

"And they left you, like Penelope at the loom waiting for Whittaker to return?"

She shot him a venomous look. "I wouldn't put it like that."

"How else would you describe it then? Something here doesn't add up for me, Leslie. You had feelings for Whittaker. Had, as in past history. Correct?"

"Correct."

"Whittaker brings a Nazi here. He thinks the man will get him closer to a coin, but he sings a different song. Whittaker was working the Russians for a private score, and then Brits show up at the party. In what world does that make any sense? Whittaker leaves with them and the German canary. The Nazi is found dead in the nuthouse, and Whittaker's place was tossed like the Cossacks saw a menorah in the window. How am I'm doing so far, Leslie?"

She said nothing.

"Here is the thing, Leslie. Your cat Mr. Meows left his fur all over the Nazi's pants. I have a safety-deposit key and writing from Whittaker's place that looks similar to yours. Care to explain that to me?"

She looked as if Joe Louis had delivered a blow to her chin.

"Say something."

"No matter what I say, it looks bad."

"I'll say. For someone good with languages, now is not the time to remain silent. You're in a grade-A mess."

"No need to remind me."

"But I will. Allow me to let you in on something, Miss Leslie from Shaker Heights. We don't say 'waistcoat.' We say 'vest.' We make our sevens the provincial way, without the slash, and our ones, they are straight up and down stick figures, not with a little hook on the top, because we're simple folks from the Colonies. It's mathematics, not 'maths.' We don't say 'lads' either. Men are men or they're boys, simple as that."

He tapped ash over the ashtray on the table. He missed.

"You're not one of us, are you?" he said. "I mean you're not an American. I learned that after I fished the package out of a toilet—wait, I meant loo. Which is it?"

"Which is what?" she said, her voice thick with emotion."

"Who do you work for? Is it MI5, or MI6? I can never get the numbers right."

Leslie seethed. "Get out."

"Gladly," he said from behind his last cloud of smoke. He walked to the door, stopped, looked down at the orange cat, on his back and cute in a pornographic way. He stopped at the door and said, "Any last words before I leave?"

"I work for the British. My reports go to Meeks."

Chapter Twenty-Four

Walker reached for the glass on his nightstand. He sat up in bed and drank the water. He replayed a transcript of his conversation with Leslie in his head. He rose and paced and checked and re-checked his space. He checked the edge of the mattress where he had put Grable.

Something was off. He knew it like some people can sense a storm in the air. They could look at the sky, or say their bones or lungs told them rain was coming. He was certain as sunrise and sunset that something was about to happen.

He returned to his bed for more self-loathing. He reviewed the facts.

Leslie had not shown up at the office for two days. A few days more of that and they both could pretend nothing had happened. There was work to do. Nazis had to be reviewed, interviewed, and fast-tracked for what they knew about Soviet technology.

Whittaker was AWOL, MIA, possibly KIA.

He rethought all that she had said about him. He could've lived in apartment on Main Street, earned his keep at some nine-to-five job for forty hours a week. His life could have been a Rockwell painting with apple pie, a cup of coffee, and conversations at the drugstore counter, a life on the buckle of the Bible Belt, where everyone in town knew everybody's business from cradle to grave, and for generations. That wouldn't have worked for him, though, because he had no interest in surrounding himself with minds as wide as a playing card.

His eyes were tired, exhausted from the walk through the minefields of memory.

He drifted, into sleep, wonderful sleep. He dreamt of that day in class when he recited Keats's *Ode to a Nightingale*. His eyelids flickered.

The ceiling fan above him sent down rhythmic waves of cool air, one after another. No matter the season, Walker preferred to sleep in a cold room. As his eyes closed his body sank into the mattress, his feet outside the sheet as if he were in the morgue.

Silence. Absolute silence.

Air raked across his toes.

He swung his arm over to the side, came up with Grable and squeezed the trigger.

Walker heard the thump, the sound of a body thrown against the wall.

He reached for the pebbled chain, pulled it. The light came on.

He discovered a dead short man.

Out of bed now, he pointed Grable at two live guests in the room with him. There was a Brit and a tall European in a dark suit, both with their weapons drawn. It was three men in a formation, Walker at the apex, and the other two formed the two bases of a triangle. One against two, and two against one, in a stalemate. Walker noticed the toothpick in the tall man's mouth. His partner spoke, "Put down the gun." The voice belonged to a young kid with the oddest taste in clothes. Walker noticed the hands, too, how his nails were polished and filed. "Put the gun down," he repeated. "Be reasonable."

Walker held his stance. "Talk."

The Brit stepped forward, arms held out wide. "Walker," he said.

The European lowered his arm and weapon, like the second hand on a tight clock, slow and steady. He kept the toothpick tight between his lips. Walker calculated his odds. His finger touched the magazine release, and with his other hand caught the clip and tossed it. The Brit caught it. Walker kept his arm and Grable extended. The Brit showed some bad teeth with his smile, the other thug lightened up on his toothpick, and Walker smiled, too, before he pulled the trigger.

Grable had pressed the dark European suit against the far wall.

The face went from pale to dead white, eyes wide open. Toothpick in place.

Walker said, "Never forget the one in the chamber."

Walker didn't see it, but the Brit brained him with a slapper.

Chapter Twenty-Five

A blackness greeted him when he opened his eyes. His hands were tied behind his back, and a rigid chairback pinched his shoulder blades together. The jacket from his apartment lay on the floor. The hood over his head made him look like a medieval falcon. He waited for his handler.

He heard voices. He recognized one of them as the Brit who had hit him. Walker squirmed to test the ties, he clenched and unclenched his jaw to assess any other damage. He was convinced they kicked him a few times during the transit because he felt sore all over.

Fingers grabbed some of the hood and his hair with it. His eyes blinked against the glare of the light overhead. Opposite him, the Brit who had sapped him, paced, an unlit cigarette stuck to his lower lip. The man who had removed the hood was wearing black slacks, a red silk shirt, Slim Jim tie, and something small and Masonic dangled from a watch chain from his pants. Sideburns crawled down both sides of his face. The man's jacket reminded Walker of the Pachucos he'd seen in Los Angeles, similar for style but different ethnic group. His head leaned down to meet Walker's face. "Fancy a fag?"

"Why not."

The man peeled back one side of his coat. Walker saw the white butt of a small revolver,. Walker was fed an Old Joe as the other hand sought a lighter or match. The tip of Walker's tongue found familiarity in the taste and feel of a cigarette between his lips. Nine cigarettes were standard field rations for him and his men. A fire lit the cigarette. His brain lifted like a rocket from the nicotine for breakfast.

Walker noticed the tattoos, the matching right and left angel wings in dark black ink on the hands. Walker took in another puff and released gray smoke.

"My colleague and I were hoping you could help us."

The walls to the room exhibited a nice curve to them.

His host noticed. "You're inside one of the gasometers."

"Good to know," Walker said.

"We'd like to review some information with you."

"My memory isn't reliable since you tried open brain surgery on me."

"Let's do this the cooperative way. You might not like the way we restore your memory."

"And what exactly is it you think I know?"

The game was underway now. At least they were polite enough to let him enjoy some of his cigarette. A hand removed the cig. Walker licked his lips.

"You're interviewing former Nazis for your government. We'd like for you to share any information you have about them and some Russians."

"Can't say I know any Russians." Walker stated the truth.

"Let us play show and tell. I will show you pictures and you tell me what you know."

His partner handed him a folder. Walker was shown photograph after black-and-white photograph. Some of the faces were German officers in uniform and others in civilian clothes, grainy and about as clear as a wet postcard left to dry on a radiator. Some were faces he had interviewed, while others were leads.

When Walker said he didn't recognize any of the faces, his chair was pulled back on its rear legs, the hood came up and over his head. At the chair's angle, the material was tight against his face like somebody was straining his face through cheesecloth. Walker knew this recipe.

He caught a few breaths through the taut material before the cold water crashed down. He inhaled some of the wetness, but the tight material rendered him unable to cough, unable to catch a full breath of air.

Walker choked on water that went down the wrong way. He gagged and coughed. The coughing transitioned into spasms of fire in his chest and lungs. His shoulder blades ached. The retching had begun and he wanted to vomit.

The chair slammed forward. His head fell forward.

The hood was pulled up enough to expose his mouth and nose.

A voice visited his left ear. "Remember anything now?"

When he didn't answer, the hood came down and his body went back in the chair. More water came, and more of it slid down his throat and up his nose. He wished he could breathe like a fish. A nastiness visited the back of his mouth. He thought this was what the inmate inside the gas chamber experienced, except there was no sweet smell of almonds to precede the agonies of suffocation. The chair smashed forward. The hood came off.

Walked made a small mess on the front of his shirt like a baby without his bib. He shook his head to free himself of water and snot. He had to breathe.

In a chair in front of him sat Meeks.

Walker's eyes squeezed tight, opened, squeezed again and focused.

It was Meeks.

"Hello again," the man said over his hands on top of a walking stick. The cane was either another affectation or one of those sword canes from a Victorian novel. Walker had nothing in his mouth to spit at the man.

"I had hoped that this could've been avoided. Torture is an altogether unreliable method for information. You impressed me with your uncanny talent for details at our meetings, so imagine my disappointment that you remember nothing now." Meeks made that annoying click with his tongue that schoolmasters did when they handed out test results to their students.

Walker sat there like a wet dog. Meeks wore a blue Savile Row suit and a Wanamaker ascot. On his pinky there was an onyx ring with a diamond, which some said was masculine, but Walker thought ridiculous.

"Why?" Walker asked.

"Why am I interested in Nazis? For the same reasons you are."

Meeks pulled out a pack of cigarettes from his pocket and waved it up and down to see whether Walker had an interest. He wasn't. His lungs had acquired a new appreciation for clean air. Walker read the brand: Windsor

Castle.

Meeks retrieved his lighter from a breast pocket. It was an electric starter in tortoise. Walker had heard about these lighters. They ran on Naptha instead of compressed butane.

Meeks spoke after he lit his cigarette. "The slogan for these cigarettes was, 'Twenty cents for twenty extra-long fags.'"

Walker responded. "I would've thought you smoked Virginia Rounds."

Meek shot him a disdainful look at the reference to women's cigarettes.

"No need to be rude." He exhaled a cloud, "Let us remain civilized."

"Next time we have tea, I'll bring my manners."

"About these Nazis."

"Who signs your check, Meeks? Sure as hell it isn't anyone in Washington."

The man placed his leg over the opposite knee. It was something Walker could appreciate in a woman but found feminine in a man.

"Talk to me about Nazis," Meeks said.

"I don't have anything to say to you."

"We have other methods, much less pleasant methods."

"Like what? You want me to breathe through my ears this time?"

Walker watched one of the Brits approach but Meek raised his hand. "No need. We'll get what we need from Mr. Marshall. Go outside, enjoy a cigarette, while I talk to our friend here."

"Best of luck with Jack," Walker said. "He is a tougher customer than I am."

The man leaned over and spoke into Walker's ear. "Oh, I don't think so. See, you're the tail of the dog, he is the head, and I have every intention of lopping the head off. I may have had my moment in the sun, but I learned that tactic during my time in Shanghai at the Great World Hotel. I want to know what else is in that book Mr. Marshall read from at our meeting, and I'll accomplish my objective, with or without you."

Walker blinked. "And your concern over Whittaker—was that all smoke?"

The Brit returned from his smoke break with a friend and with a surprise for Walker. They entered the room with Whittaker. Walker tried to hide his surprise. Whittaker looked like fruit gone bad. Bruised and banged about, he had one black eye.

Meeks filled Walker in. "My boys crossed paths with him while they conducted interviews of our own. It's amazing how former Nazis unburdened themselves to anyone who would listen, American or British. Russians troops around Vienna will do that. Whittaker led us to the unfortunate fellow in the asylum." Meeks looked over to Whittaker standing between his dogs. "It seems your friend romanced your girl. Don't think I didn't notice how you look at Leslie."

"You're scum, Meeks."

Meeks grinned. "And I have one more surprise for you two." He whistled.

In walked a terrified Leslie with a chaperone. He guided her by the arm with all the delicacy of a longshoreman at a cotillion. Leslie had been roughed up, manhandled. She was brought over to Meeks.

He placed his hands on her shoulders and screwed her down into an available chair. "Leslie works for the Secret Intelligence Service. You know, MI6."

Walker watched her look down at the floor.

"British intelligence planted her in your office. They sent a woman to do a man's job."

Meeks stroked her hair as he would a loyal pet. "She supplied me with updates on you and Jack because she realized I had the goods on Whittaker. Imagine that, she has a soft spot for the brute. I asked her to give me information on you, but, unlike most men, you don't talk about your work."

Leslie's cheeks were scarlet with humiliation. Her eyes told a different story. Rage.

"One of you will tell me what was on those typewriter ribbons, but I have an easier question first. Where are they?"

Not hearing a response, he put his hand down Leslie's blouse. Leslie looked as if iced water had been dumped on her. A Brit pinned Whittaker against the wall. Leslie bit her lip.

"The typewriter ribbons. Where are they?"

"I don't know," she said.

"That's a shame." Meeks removed his hand. He pulled out a handkerchief and wiped his hand as if her skin had contaminated it.

Leslie sprang up, but before she could say or do a thing, he backhanded her hard. She landed like wet laundry near Walker's feet. Leslie stumbled to her knees and wiped away the blood from her lips.

"You bastard," she said. "And you," she directed her voice at the British thugs. "You disgust me."

"Sit down," Meeks said.

Meeks motioned to one of his men. He grabbed her by a wrist and forced her into her chair. Meeks and the man stepped aside to talk. Walker watched their lips move. Gnats at a summer picnic made more noise. Meeks left, and this spelled a change of plans, or worse. The man Meeks spoke with was in charge

"Disgust you, do we Miss?" He looked over to his crony to confirm he had a firm hold on Whittaker. He yanked Leslie up and turned the chair around. The back of the chair faced Walker. Leslie looked confused. The man issued his instruction, "Get on your knees on that chair, now."

Leslie, uncertain what he intended, took hold of the back of the chair with her hands. She knelt on the seat. The man's hand reached under her skirt from behind.

Whittaker struggled but two guards pressed him harder into the brick wall.

Walker could hear Leslie's undergarments tear. The two thugs holding Whittaker seem surprised. One of them said, "What are you doing, mate?"

Leslie's assailant ignored him. His hand hooked over Leslie's hip and it was no mystery what his other hand was doing or about to do. Leslie shut her eyes tight. She shuddered as he thrusted himself inside her. The man rutted a few times until he found a rhythm. He flashed his British comrades the Churchill victory sign. When he turned his head away from them a bullet ripped through his head. He toppled over dead, without too much of his brains, onto the floor. One of the Brits had killed the rapist.

The shooter lowered his gun. The two men didn't seem to mind seeing Whittaker rush forward to comfort Leslie. The man with the weapon said, "Don't go thinking we're all friends now. We've got business to do." He considered the dead man on the floor. "This one here was never right in the head."

Whittaker said, "I'll take you to where I have the typewriter ribbons."

"You can do that?"

"I can." Whittaker helped Leslie to standing. "But I need his help."

"Why?"

"You'll understand when we get there."

"His hands stay tied, understand?" the gunman said.

Whittaker nodded. Whittaker freed Walker from the chair and, without the two goons seeing it, loosened his restraints enough that with a little more work Walker could free himself on his own.

"We need a car," Whittaker said.

"There's one outside," the man said.

One of the Brits motioned Leslie towards the door. His partner nudged Whittaker and Walker to follow her. Whittaker picked up Walker's suit jacket and handed it to him.

In the dark passage from the gasometer to the car, Walker felt a heaviness inside his jacket. One of the men held the door open for her. "Miss, you get in the rear."

"Whittaker, in front with us," the man in charge said.

"C'mon, we don't have all night," the voice said their driver. Whittaker sat between the two men in the front seat. He turned briefly and looked to Leslie and Walker. He smiled at them as the car engine turned over. He looked down at Walker's jacket before he turned around and faced front.

The car moved out onto the main road. Walker's shoulders ached. Leslie slipped her right hand into Walker's pocket. She found the small gun that Whittaker had slipped into Walker's jacket. The thugs had failed to frisk him.

As the car picked up speed, she eased the firearm out and she pushed down the safety lever. While Walker worked his hands free, Leslie pulled the weapon up and snapped off two shots. The first one went into the back of the driver's head. She swung the weapon over to the passenger side and sent the second round into the passenger's face. The car swerved off the road, down an embankment, and turned over.

Their car upside down, she helped Walker undo the last of his restraints before she crawled out of the vehicle. The wheels of the car were still turning when Walker extricated himself from the wreck. They surveyed the scene together. Leslie was the first to see the unnatural angle of Whittaker's neck. Eerie and macabre as Whittaker looked in death, there was a final smile of contentment across his face.

The diminutive Colt .380 Whittaker had slipped him was a final act of friendship, a final penance, and it made the car ride a Todestrieb or 'death drive.'

Chapter Twenty-Six

They came to Simmeringer Hauptstrasse, the central crematorium of Vienna.

After Whittaker's cremation and while they waited for the cremains, Walker stood outside to take in the weather and the solemnity of the occasion. The trees had shed their leaves, their branches, bare but with an abundance of crows on them. A bird emitted a loud shriek before it took flight.

With Leslie, they had watched the coffin slide on a conveyor through a window in the wall. They witnessed the modest roar of flames that waited for their friend. A door closed. Like Whittaker's life and death, it was over quickly. A life, a flame, and ashes. Jack received the urn.

He joined Walker outside. "Thought you'd be having a cigarette."

"I've quit the habit after the gasometer."

Jack looked in the direction of the Company vehicle. "Let's sit inside the car and talk."

"What about Leslie?"

"I asked her to give us a few minutes."

Inside the car, Jack placed the urn between them.

"How is she, Jack?"

"She needs to recover from the shock of what happened to her."

"Shock? That's some euphemism, Jack."

"What do you want me to say? It's an unfortunate possibility with women as colleagues."

"What's your position on her in the office, now that you know?"

"Know what?" His eyes forward, Jack said, "That she works for the British? I knew."

"You knew? And you have no problem with the open window?"

"I had my suspicions, but I wasn't certain."

"Until the note from Whittaker's place, the writing?"

"That, I knew it's a common practice."

"What is?" Walker asked.

"Our Allies want to know our business, and we want to know theirs."

"Agencies spy on each other, is that it?" Walker said.

"Think of it as keeping each other on our toes, but Meeks has turned this into something different."

"Whatever she told him, Jack, it wasn't enough, Meeks is after the file you read to him, like you said, and he is hot for those typewriter ribbons?"

"She told me she fed him status reports, and nothing more."

Walker asked, "She say anything as to what is his endgame might be?"

"She said she didn't know."

"And you believe her. You've got to admit it, Jack. She is a great actress. She convinced everyone she was an American. What's your take on her and Whittaker?"

"It happens in the field. We're all human."

"Meeks asked me about Nazis, but do you think he's after the coin?"

Jack stared through the windshield. "It's possible. I'd like to think he is interested in the Russian behind the coin."

"This is a mess."

"Speaking of messes, I had cleaners take care of the car, and the bodies. I'll have them visit your place soon."

"And what happens when Meeks figures out his goons didn't come home?"

"I have eyes on the Sacher."

"Meeks wants those ribbons, Jack."

"And my notebook from the meeting, I know."

"Any chance Meeks was telling the truth, that Whittaker had the ribbons?"

Jack mused. "You did find a key at his place, and we never matched it to anything."

"You don't think she could be in on it, do you?"

"The ribbons, no. The coin, maybe."

Walker looked over to Jack, saw the profile, and those eyes that he'd seen numerous times, the eyes that reviewed the battlefield before the casualties, before the engagement. Walked waited for the officer inside Jack Marshall to talk, and he did.

"Until Meeks learns his grunts are MIA, he'll assume that you, Leslie, and Whittaker are dead, which leaves me vulnerable. He knows I'll start looking for you, asking questions, and he may suspect that I'll put in a request for an investigation. Meeks won't like that, especially if it reaches Karlsruhe, but an ask like that starts with Davies."

Chapter Twenty-Seven

The phone announced reveille. He rolled and pulled the receiver to his ear. "Yes?"

"Meet me at Schlossstrasse, sobald wie möglich."

Walker rubbed his face. He had heard the 'as soon as you can' in German, but asked, "Please be specific. It's a long street, Jack."

"Corner of Grunbergstrasse, near the Meidlinger Gate." The line clicked.

Walker told himself that these calls, this life, the work, they either built character or would turn him into one. He dressed, half drowsy and half angry. He passed the razor over his face and used a comb to shape the landscape that was his hair after he brushed his teeth. He was thinking that he could use some coffee, like most people, to get his feet on the first floor of the day, when he realized that Grable was gone, thanks to the bad guys in the middle of the night.

The day began jinxed.

* * *

Jack shoved a cup of coffee into Walker's hand. Walker thought that the Viennese, who had a rich history of coffee culture, must consider the concept of takeaway coffee a form of barbarism, suitable only for Americans.

"Follow me," Jack said, as he walked over to a group of men in jumpsuits. Jack presented his identification and informed them that Walker was with him. One of the men took a pickaxe and opened up the sewer covering. Another man handed Jack and Walker a pair of boots each. The sewer police awaited them below Schlossstrasse.

Down into the darkness they descended. An unholy stench greeted them.

Walker recognized the Inspector from the night of the dead Nazi at the asylum. The man issued quick, firm orders to his men before he approached Jack and Walker. The Inspector looked down at the coffee in Walker's hand. Walker raised the cup. "Coffee is what makes mornings better."

"You have a report for us?" Jack asked.

"In your choice of German, French, Russian, or English. Come with me."

Walker watched a rat paddle through the water and lift itself onto dry land before it disappeared into the darkness. Sewer police were gathered at the water's edge around something in the distance.

The Inspector asked Jack, "Major General Davies, isn't he one of your men?"

"A colleague, yes, why?" Jack's eyes searched the area around the jumpsuits.

"And what is it that you and the General do?"

"He helps me run an Assurance Company."

The Inspector kept his hands behind his back. "I always did admire a good lie. Please have a look." The Inspector's nod included Walker.

They walked to the water's edge. The sewer police stepped away and the lump under a draw sheet came into view. Jack asked an officer to pull the sheet.

It was clear that Major General Davies had been dead for some time; his corpse had become bloated from its time in the water.

"Looks like he struggled," Jack said.

"You can see defensive marks on his hands," the Inspector said. "He fought off a man with a knife. There are stab wounds to his abdomen, defensive wounds on his forearms."

Jack added his own analysis. "And a second man strangled him from behind, which explains why his torso was exposed to a knife attack."

The eyes were closed. The sewer police probably closed them out of respect for the deceased. Jack borrowed a flashlight from one of the officers. Blood vessels on the face and scalp had burst, consistent with strangulation. Jack found an uneven ligature around the throat.

Walker lost interest in his coffee and emptied it, away from the scene.

The Inspector said, "Our physician will inform me if there is water in his lungs or not."

Jack rose from his catcher's stance. "A knife wasn't used to stab him."

"Are you sure?" Walker asked.

"Ice pick."

The Inspector asked Jack and Walker to step away so he could have a private word with them. "I am willing to drag my feet a little, shuffle paperwork from one side of my desk to the other, but I ask that you resolve this matter quickly." He looked to Jack and then Walker. "It's my understanding that you two had a meeting at the Hotel Sacher."

"Seems Vienna has eyes," Jack said.

The Inspector smiled. "A man named Meeks resides at the Sacher."

"Vienna listens, too. Remind me to get my hearing checked," Walker said.

"And this Mr. Meeks, I assume there is no love for the man?"

"About as much as hydrogen loves a spark," Jack said. He looked to the corpse. "I'd like to arrange for this man's remains after the examiner completes his report."

The Inspector nodded. The man moved in closer to Jack. "Resolve this sooner than later, please. I have to prepare a statement for the Consulate. The sewer police found him, so they have their own paperwork."

"You said you could drag your feet a bit, but what about the police?" Jack asked.

"Papers are known to be lost, misplaced."

"How much time before this reaches the Consulate."

"No more than forty-eight hours," the Inspector said and walked away.

Jack and Walker were alone with the body.

"How did he know about the meeting at the Sacher?" Walker asked.

"Sometimes God gives us our mysteries with both hands."

Chapter Twenty-Eight

Jack drank an espresso straight, followed by a shot of whiskey. The Viennese boilermaker.

The world had grown more complicated since his boyhood days of fly-fishing in Montana, days when he'd cast his line into the water of a river and where his biggest decision would be the choice of either to use dry fly or streamer. Life then was a matter of technique and compassion. There was technique in angling and compassion in catch and release.

Hatred he had learned when he had to shotgun black-tailed jackrabbits. He understood respect the day he turned a corner in the Bitterroot Mountains and realized that a Canada lynx could have killed him but had spared him instead.

Herding had taught Jack how to be the man Jack Marshall. It wasn't the harsh sun or big sky that had done it. It was knowing when to act decisive with the thousand pounds of horse under him and thousands more around him. Instinct had to kick in before his horse panicked if it smelled blood in the air, and hysteria infected the herd and forced it to stampede.

Jack took a sip and then a shot.

In front of him on the desk were the money, the note, and the mysterious key from Whittaker's place. The money meant nothing to him, and the note seemed superfluous.

The key is what interested him the most. He wondered whether there was a connection between the key and the missing ribbons, since Whittaker had hidden one in a toilet, mentioned the other at the gasometer.

The whiskey worked his brain and the espresso paced his heart. He stared at the shape of the key. The shank ended in teeth and ridges looked like the spur gears used to wind a clock.

Jack decided that he would go to the Erste Bank and try his luck there for a match. Pandora's box had already been opened in Vienna, with one dead Nazi, some thugs, and now, Major General Davies.

The world was changing. He saw it and he read it everywhere.

There was talk of Commies in the universities, Commies in town meetings, subversives within the government, immoral elements hard at work like weevils on the fabric of the American way of life, although nobody had bothered to define or describe the condition of the fabric.

Jack thought of the bald eagle, the country's symbol, when he looked at the key from Whittaker's apartment. He could imagine the day that rather than holding arrows in one talon, the bird would be clutching a turnkey for atomic missiles. He could see a paper with launch codes instead of a sprig of laurel in the other claw.

He walked across the room and fiddled with the radio dial. He needed some distraction. He hoped to find something over the airwaves from the other side of the world. He turned the dial, like a safecracker, to find the English-speaking world. He did find something.

Ed Fleming bubbled on about an insecticide, some bug-killer. Jack could use some of that in Vienna but his bugs were bigger than the ones Mr. Fleming said he had under his floorboards. After Ed came some gossip hounds who said Hollywood was nothing more than a boomtown of weirdoes and degenerates. They talked pools and palm trees. He'd like some of that water and shade himself. Then the newshounds bayed that Communists were stealing the soft life and the sunshine.

A Lifebuoy Health Soap ad came and went. The organ chime and the announcer's voice said it was time for Jack Webb as Jeff Regan, Investigator. The evening's episode was *Pilgrim's Progress*.

The episode passed over Jack's ears for the half hour it lasted. He stared at the ceiling, loosened his tie some. He counted progress in Vienna. There were three dead men in a car made to look like an accident. There was one dead Nazi in a nuthouse. And now dear Davies, dead among sewer scum and vermin. After everything Davies had survived, he had to die like that. That wasn't right. The way Davies had died offended Jack's sense of decency. An obscenity.

Jack unbuttoned the top button to his shirt. He missed Bitterroot River and Lolo Creek. He remembered his first and only 22-inch trout. The river was clear and ran with riffles and nobody thought about the water ahead of them or behind them, because what mattered most was the cast where a fly fisherman stood. The sky was so open and so pure a man could breathe through his eyes.

And then it hit him. Jack almost fell off his bed when he reached for the phone. He dialed Walker's exchange. The line rang and rang. "Pick up, Walker. Pick up the damn phone."

Then, the clang and bang of receiver meant someone was there.

"Walker, I need you to listen to me."

"For cripe's sake, Jack, have you any idea what—"

"He's closing the circle."

"Who is closing what circle, Jack?"

"Meeks."

Jack had hoped that the one-syllable name would awaken Walker, that it'd ring bright between his ears as if the man's silver set were dropped on the floor. He wanted Walker up and out of his bed.

The whiskey and espresso had met and opened a highway in his mind.

"You need to find Leslie. He needs to cross her off his list. Did you hear me?"

"I heard you," Walker said.

"One more thing."

"What is it?"

"Under the mattress, on the right side, cut into the webbing of the box spring. There's something there for you from the cleaners. I'll contact you later. Viel Glück."

'Good luck' and the line went dead.

Walker followed Jack's instructions. After Whittaker's death, Jack had professionals visit his place and remove any trace evidence of the shooting before he'd been kidnapped. They went over his apartment with the patience of a Zen Master with a garden rake. He cut into the box spring.

He was stunned.

It was Grable.

Chapter Twenty-Nine

"May I help you?" she said from behind the counter of the Erste, the oldest bank in Vienna.

Mascara across the eyelids like Cleopatra, she was tall, her hair pulled back, and in a blue suit that said she was the manager. The lips in red lipstick suggested few victims escaped her. This woman was all instinct and business.

"I have a safety-deposit key."

Her eyes scanned for respectability. Jack heard himself breathe while she decided how long she would make him wait. Clocks on the wall told time in Switzerland, New York, Chicago, and far away San Francisco.

"This way, please."

He followed her. Her feet moved, her body sashayed in a way that might make most women forget about the men in the room. She walked head held high.

Keys on a ring shivered. The lock turned, and bars moved across marble. She was the warden to money condemned to solitary confinement inside the vault. Jack was thinking that the subterranean tomb was on the same level as the Viennese sewers.

"Feel free to use one of the private rooms over there." Her eyes indicated a row of rooms with doors covered with thick bottle glass for privacy. He thanked her, but she stood there and Jack had no choice but to walk around her.

Jack searched the wall of the metallic crypt. He read numbers and found the one that matched his key. He inserted his key and she appeared next to him with her matching key necessary to open the box. Two keys, one turn, and he slid the security box out from the wall.

"I'll give you some privacy," she said.

The box was not heavy. Jack put it under his arm and took it with him into a private room. He closed the door. The space was functional and Swiss in its lack of personality.

Under the white light, he lifted the lid and viewed the contents.

Whittaker's dog tags.

Medals, and letters of commendation from the War, including one from Jack.

Some newspaper clippings from the States.

No ribbons, but there was something else there.

Jack picked it up. It was real, very real. He held it and then placed it into his side pocket. He tapped his jacket again. The world had just gotten complicated and simpler all at once. He closed the lid, went over to the wall and slid the safe-deposit box into its slot for the ages.

Jack was Fred Astaire because he had music and dance in his feet. So happy was Jack Marshall that he gave the long-legged lady bank manager a peck on the cheek. She didn't mind the affection. Jack was a married man but, for a second, adulterous thoughts of her seemed worth an eternity in Perdition.

Chapter Thirty

The diner was on the same street as Sheldon's tailor shop. The menu was on simple, easy-to-read and easier-to-clean laminated stock. The text was legible, the words on the page included a dropped 'a' from the Underwood typewriter used to type the bill of fare. The front side described everything Walker expected from a diner back home. The reverse listed drinks. The house coffee was black as hell and bottomless as a mother's love. There was not a word in German.

Leslie was at his side, and Grable was under his arm.

She hunted for something healthy. The place was busy, home to a hundred conversations and a thousand thoughts. A pair of women sat near them, gossiping. A man at another table mopped his balding head and then the back of his neck. Walker's hand reached for hers but she swatted it away and told him that she had not made up her mind. He said that he was trying to get her to look at the Wurlitzer Peacock jukebox against the wall.

Jack slid into the booth opposite them and hailed the waitress. A handsome girl idled up to the table in a blue and white striped dress, white apron around small hips. A white bowtie on top of her head held her hair prisoner. She spoke English as clear as Libbey Rock Sharpe crystal.

Leslie ordered two eggs over easy with a side of wheat toast and coffee. Walker surrendered his menu after he requested pancakes with two eggs over easy, three bacon strips, and coffee. Jack wasted no time with his decision. He chose three eggs over easy, three strips of smoked bacon, three sausages and two slices of country ham, with black coffee. The waitress scribbled the orders in restaurant shorthand, with a short pencil, a few touches from the tip with her tongue on her small notepad. She collected their menus and departed. Leslie stared at Jack,

"You plan to have a cigarette after that coronary for a breakfast?"

"No, Mother, I will not. I leave any smoking to Walker."

"You're chipper than a rooster in the henhouse."

"I'm in too good of a mood for anyone to spoil it. And how are you, dear?"

Leslie looked surprised that Jack had called her 'mother' and 'dear.'

Walker spoke. "You okay over there? And, for the record, I gave up smoking. How did you know about this place?"

"Saw it when I visited Sheldon's shop."

Their waitress returned with their dishes, and another waitress poured coffee. They ate in silence until Leslie broke it. "Walker told me about Davies, and he says you're concerned about my safety." When she finished her breakfast, she crossed her knife and fork on her plate. "He mentioned Meeks but didn't give me details."

"Meeks wants to control any information that goes to Karlsruhe, now that Davies is dead."

Walker added, "And Jack is convinced that Meeks thinks we're dead."

Jack spoke. "Meeks knows Whittaker and his goons are dead, which puts him on the move. I had the details to the car accident put in any papers he might find, so that buys us time. You two find a new place?"

Walker said, "Innere Stadt, a quaint out-of-the-way neighborhood."

Jack stopped to appreciate his breakfast. "This food makes me miss home." The moment faded fast, and he returned to business like a revenue man. "Leslie, I need to know what you told Meeks in those reports."

"I already told you."

"Tell me again," Jack said.

"The ins and outs of the office, and nothing more. None of it deviates from anything any of the other secretaries might've filed. To do otherwise would arouse suspicion."

"Did Meeks know about you and Whittaker?"

"He knew, yes."

"And the coin?" Jack asked.

"He knew Whittaker was chasing it, and that he got himself in with some Russians."

"Is it possible he knew about the coin and the Russians from another source?" Jack's fork worked on the blunt end of a sausage.

"I don't know, and that's the God's honest truth, Jack."

Jack's plate was as white as eyes before summer allergies. "I ask because the men at the gasometer were British."

She said, "And you think they were British intelligence."

"Were they?" Jack asked.

"No."

"Recognize them?"

"No, and they weren't in form."

"Form?" Jack was taken back. "I don't understand."

"They were dressed like scuttlers." She saw Jack's confused look, so she explained. "In northern England, especially in Manchester, there are neighborhood gangs, rowdy types with distinctive clothes. They fancied themselves as the poor man's Neil Munro. These two dressed like him, except their hair was longer."

Jack interrupted. "Who is Neil Munro?"

"British Rifle Brigade."

"A war hero?"

"And a colorful bon vivant," Leslie added.

"Munro was a connoisseur, and these punks are rogue elements?" Jack counted money to pay the bill.

"Munro was an art connoisseur, among other indulgences," Leslie answered.

"Think these scuttlers at the gasometer were into art, like Munro? I ask because my contact at the police says they're enrolled at the Courtauld Institute of Art at the University of London."

"Are you thinking they're MI5?" Walker asked.

"MI5 is domestic. MI6 is foreign intelligence," Leslie said.

Walker absorbed the edit.

"I'm more interested in their connection to Meeks, but I have a theory,"

Jack said.

Leslie said, "Care to elaborate?"

"Private muscle. They do his dirty work, and if Meeks is after art for his private collection, he gives them a finder's fee. The coin is worth money to collectors. Of course, there's another possibility," Jack said. "It's a Russian coin, so Meeks could be interested in the Russian behind the coin. You've dealt with the man, Leslie. What are your thoughts?"

"I don't know. He might be after the coin for himself, like you said."

"And my theory about interest in any Russians behind the coin?"

"If Meeks is patriotic, he'd flip a Russian for intel."

"Agree." Jack nodded. "Did Meeks squeeze you hard for info on Whittaker?"

"If by squeeze, you mean blackmail, then yes."

"What leverage could Meeks possibly have on you?" Walker asked.

"Fear of being sacked," she said.

"For fraternization?" Walker hated to use the word. "Your affair was in the past."

"Doesn't matter," Leslie said. "Double standard. I have a question for you two."

Jack looked up and waited.

"How did Meeks know I was MI6 before I arrived in Vienna?"

"Davies, I presume," Jack answered.

"Or someone in the Home Office told him," Leslie said.

"Where is home, officially?" Walker asked.

"London." Leslie said. "Look, to be clear, I never compromised any interviews. My notes were no different than the minutes or anything that any secretary in the office typed up."

Jack smiled. "You made that clear the first time."

Walker said, "It would explain why Meeks was eager to see your notes at the meeting."

Leslie said, "He must've felt I was holding out on him."

"Enough to have someone break into the office and steal the ribbons?" Jack said.

Walker sat back. "If he had the ribbons, then why would he need your notes, Jack?"

"Wanted to know everything?"

Leslie said over her cold coffee, "We can conjecture all day. What do you propose now?"

Jack's hand reached into his side pocket. He placed it on the table, his hand over it. Walker and Leslie waited for Jack the magician. Jack moved his hand and there against the green speckled tabletop was the silver coin. Jack covered it up and slid the coin beneath the table and into his pocket. "That was a Constantine, and I believe it's the minter's personal coin. Whittaker had it in a safe-deposit box."

"Any ribbons in the box with it?" Walker asked.

"No ribbons."

"Hate to sound like an echo, but what do we do now?" Leslie asked.

Jack gave an answer. "With Davies dead, Karlsruhe will scramble to install his replacement, and that isn't me. I doubt it'll be Meeks. Like I said earlier, Meeks thinks you two are dead, but when he finds out you're not, he'll send his men after you because he knows you have dirt on him. Since we don't know who else works for him, you two need to lay low in Innere Stadt."

Leslie asked, "What do you think he'll do to buy time?"

Jack answered, "He'll say you went rogue."

"That I went rogue?" Leslie said.

"He'll spin that double standard for all the gold it's worth. I wouldn't be surprised if he put the two of you into his report to the brass at MI6."

Leslie looked hurt. "He'll use Walker's name to insinuate that I am a whore?"

"This is Meeks we're talking about," Jack said. "You two hide, while I draw him out."

Walker said it. "You're left alone and vulnerable."

"I'm neither alone nor vulnerable. I have Sheldon."

Chapter Thirty-One

The door in front of Jack was new and recently stained. He felt as if he about to vandalize a public place if he knocked on it. Under the hallway light, he saw his reflection distorted in the grain of the wood. His face was split into many Jack Marshalls. On the other side of this door lived a man, a suspected killer of Nazis, a man who had survived a horrendous nightmare of history. And here he was, Jack Marshall, about to ask him for help.

He knocked anyway. His fist made it known that he was impatient. He was. The last image he had of himself in the wood was of him as if he were some teenager anxious for his date. Beads of sweat ran down the back of his neck.

The door opened.

It was a cautious, partial revelation of face and wood. Sheldon couldn't have hidden the surprise even if he had tried. His face turned into a mask of cold formality. The two men stared at each other. Jack said it as wooden as a five-cent Indian outside the cigar shop.

"It's me, Jack Marshall."

"I remember who you are." Sheldon stood there in pressed slacks and white shirt, the sleeves pulled up, ready for some work. Jack detected the scent of sandalwood in the air.

The overhead light hummed. Their eyes locked in some kind of chess match.

"Care to come in?" Sheldon said, at last.

Jack stepped forward, hat off. He was prepared to tell the man why he had come to visit him, but Sheldon walked into the small living room. Jack saw the late breakfast on the table. The strong coffee hit his nose with a soft punch. Jack counted two settings. He did the quick look-around for a guest and saw nobody.

"I hope I didn't catch you at a bad time."

"May I offer you some coffee?"

"Uh, yes, that would be nice, thank you." Jack studied the walls, leaned back on his heels to steal a view of the bedroom, and listened for sounds of life elsewhere, but nothing. Jack thought back to what he had heard from the Bureau boys back home. They said the most efficient killers were polite and silent, sometimes very intelligent, exacting in their rituals, especially in their manners, but lethal nonetheless.

Sheldon returned with a cup and saucer in hand.

"Your jacket, please." Sheldon's hands were out for the garment.

Jack took it off and said that he was pressed for time. Jack wondered whether Sheldon asked for the coat to determine whether he was carrying or not. He was, but surrendered the jacket so Sheldon could see his weapon on his belt, in plain sight.

Jack spied books on mathematics and languages on the windowsill. He picked up what appeared to be an English composition book. Sheldon returned with his own coffee, seeing Jack with the book.

"Working on your English?" Jack said and held up the book.

"Always looking to improve myself."

"You do all right with English, if I might say so."

"You're very kind."

"You do more than all right, especially since contractions are the hardest things for non-native speakers to master."

"To what do I owe the honor of your visit, Mr. Marshall?"

Jack suspected butter and diplomacy wouldn't work on a man who had survived the Gestapo and Auschwitz. Jack adopted an honest and direct approach.

"I need your help, Sheldon. There is no other way for me to say it. Lately, I've been one of those circus seals, the one who balances the beach ball on his nose, except it's now the weight of the whole world."

"Help with what?"

"You pointed me to a Russian last time we talked."

"And you wish to speak to him again?"

"I'd like that. He educated me about one of my missing men, who as it turned out was doing his own thing on the side. The rest I had to learn the hard way. I could use his help again."

Sheldon offered Jack some fruit on a plate. "And what did you learn the hard way?"

"I learned rats swim well in Vienna. I learned that the rodent has a flexible spine. Did you know a rat can crawl into a hole the size of a quarter in a wall? Next thing you know he is listening in on all of your conversations."

Sheldon said, "And you think you have a rat problem?"

"Rats are like roaches. There is never just one."

Sheldon lowered his cup of coffee. "Sounds like you need an exterminator."

"I agree."

"You want me to rid you of vermin, Mr. Marshall?"

"Extermination I could do myself, but where I need help is drawing the rat out."

"You need a piece of cheese?" Sheldon said.

"All I need to see are his whiskers."

"And you think the General can help you?"

"Maybe he has a problem with rats?"

"And you can help him?"

"I can and I will, but time is critical."

"It always is. Tempus fugit. It's not the full quote from Virgil, but you get the gist."

Jack put the Constantine on the table. It lay there untouched.

A door creaked open. Jack sprang up, his hand on his holster. In Jack's line of sight was a blonde, a book in one hand and a pastry in the other. Jack's hand relaxed.

The girl treaded over to where Sheldon stood and put her hand on his shoulder. Jack placed his weapon and holster-clip on the table. The wood grip and blue steel contrasted against the bright silver coin. After Sheldon had said something to her in Russian, she walked into the kitchen, eyes once more on Jack before she disappeared.

Sheldon explained everything to Jack, everything from the violence that first day he met her, to her family history. He explained that the girl stayed indoors, intent on academics, with minimal trips outside. "It's too dangerous for her to venture out."

Jack offered information in trade. He detailed what had happened to Whittaker and Davies, and that Walker and Leslie were hiding, though he didn't say where. He asked Sheldon, "How long do you think you can continue what you're doing?

"Hiding her?" Sheldon said.

"Killing Nazis. It has to stop, especially now that you have a liability."

"Not that I'm admitting to anything," Sheldon said. "What do you suggest I do?"

"Leave Vienna, go to Palestine."

"As a Jew I can go to Palestine. She can't because she's not. If I hand her over to one of the child agencies here, she becomes a ward of the state and then transferred to an orphanage, which would likely be Russian. I can't let that happen. You understand why."

"The longer you have her around you, the greater the risk. She's a child, Sheldon."

"More like thirteen going on thirty."

"Arrange this meeting with the General, and I will help her. What is her name?"

"Tania."

Jack pushed the gun across the table. "Take it. You know how to use it, don't you?"

Sheldon considered the pistol.

"It's a SIG P210," Jack said. "The Swiss make more than watches and cuckoo clocks."

"That would leave you unarmed," Sheldon said.

"I have something on my ankle."

* * *

Jack suggested lunch, that the three of them visit a café on Ringstrasse, near the university. Sheldon told Tania to change into something nice. She returned wearing a dress Sheldon had bought for her, but Jack had no way of knowing it was her only dress. He offered to assist with her coat, holding it open so she could slip her arms into the sleeves. "Thank you, but I prefer it draped on my shoulders. What is the fashion in America for girls my age?"

"Sweaters over a blouse, bobby socks, and saddle shoes are popular. Plaid skirts, too."

"I hate plaid."

"Hate is a strong word, Tania," Sheldon said.

"But, I do hate plaid. And what about hairstyles, Mr. Marshall?"

"Long and pulled back."

"So my hairstyle is out of style then."

She seemed to say it with pride, as if nonconformity was her point. Jack's wife Betty had warned him that teenagers were self-conscious and 'finding themselves.' Betty lay the blame on the magazines, the movies, and hormones.

"Your hair is fine," Sheldon said.

"Does it make me look older?"

"Sophisticated is the word," Jack said, and opened the door.

* * *

The exterior of the café building was white as a wedding cake, five stories high, and the façade housed all the tiers and layers a bride and groom could want. Four wooden columns were a gateway into a lavish interior of dark wood, lush upholstery with geometric patterns, and wall panels that shone like paintings from Klimt's golden phase. Freud had taught across the street, and Mahler and Kálmán would review musical scores here.

Their table was near the window, a curtain between it and the street outside. Tania peered through the lace. For a time, the world was outside and foreign. Jack insisted she order whatever she wanted. It was lunch, but it didn't have to be lunch. She could have a starter, or several small plates. Tania looked to Sheldon for permission. She had never had smoked salmon. Sheldon looked to Jack. He nodded. Salmon was fine.

They ate their way through a course of smoked salmon for her, chanterelle salad for Sheldon, and Jack, missing home, asked for ham and cheese toast with French fries and ketchup. No one said it but they were all tired of the Viennese staples of schnitzel, goulash with bread dumplings and gherkins, and Tafelspitz, boiled beef.

The waiter cleared their dishes. Tania tapped Sheldon's leg under the table. She had noticed his interest in the waiter. The nudge was as if to say, this waiter was no Errol Flynn and he seemed stiff as the menu.

"Do you have family waiting for you in the States?" Sheldon asked.

"My wife, Betty, and our two children, Elizabeth and Jack Junior."

The waiter returned with menus for coffee and dessert.

"My Elizabeth is younger than you, Tania."

"Does she wears saddle shoes and plaid skirts?"

"Please don't be fresh, Tania," Sheldon said.

"But he said earlier that girls—never mind. I apologize, Mr. Marshall. Sarcasm was not my intention."

"To be honest, I wouldn't know," Jack said. "I haven't seen my daughter for quite some time. First, it was the war, and then I was home for a short respite, and well, now I'm here in Vienna."

Tania lowered her head. "I'm sorry to hear that. A girl must miss her father."

"Let's talk dessert, shall we?" Jack said.

Neither he nor Betty believed children should have coffee, but Europe was different. Children often enjoyed a small glass of wine with dinner. They would run errands to the corner store and purchase beer, wine, and cigarettes for their parents.

Jack read the choices on the menu. The Viennese penchant for spiked coffee, whether it was larded up with whipped cream or a spritz of favorite liqueur or spirit, was another thing Jack could never get himself accustomed to. Jack followed Sheldon's lead and ordered a strong black coffee.

Sheldon and Tania decided on warm apple strudel. Betty wasn't there to chastise him so Jack opted for decadence. He would order the chocolate almond soufflé.

"I'm sorry, sir, but we are out of the soufflé," their waiter said. "Another choice, perhaps?"

"Coffee is fine, thank you," Jack said.

Moments later, another waiter delivered their coffee.

"You should've insisted on the soufflé," Tania whispered across the table.

"They're out of it, and it's okay," Jack said.

Tania asked to be excused. Both Jack and Sheldon rose when she stood up. Jack was relieved that she had asked to visit the powder room, as it would give him time with Sheldon.

"I'll see what I can do about getting her to the States, but there's likely to be a glitch."

"What's a glitch?"

"A problem. I may not be able to get you both in together. Your entry into the US will require a little finesse."

Sheldon's head pulled back. "Is it because she's a refugee from a Communist country?"

"No."

"Is it because I'm not her father?"

"You're a Jew, and your application will draw attention if you declare yourself a survivor." Jack's hands lifted slightly and collapsed back on the table in resignation. He was about to say more, but his eyes looked across the room. Tania was holding court with two waiters. She was flirting with them. Her head was cocked back in laughter, her thumb playing with a small chain around her neck. She said her goodbyes, turned away from her admirers, and made her way back to the table. Their eyes met. She had the walk, the hip movements down cold. The only thing missing was the wink.

They rose again and she resumed her seat. A moment later her apple strudel arrived. Jack informed her that he would try and get her to the States, and it would take time. He was about to say more when a waiter interrupted.

"Your chocolate almond soufflé, sir. I misspoke earlier. Compliments of the house."

The man was gone before Jack could thank him. He looked towards Tania, but she was conveniently distracted; her hand had pulled the curtain so she could watch life on the street.

They sipped their coffees and ate their desserts.

Delighted with his soufflé, Jack said, "When I'm home, Elizabeth demands I take her to the zoo. I'd love to take you to the zoo sometime, Tania."

"The papers say the Tiergarten may reopen soon," she said. "The main attractions are three lion cubs, and a rhino."

Jack used his fork to work the last of the dessert off the plate.

"My daughter's favorite animal at the zoo is the zebra. I don't quite know why, but Betty says little girls like ponies. What do you think, Tania?"

"Perhaps Elizabeth likes the contrast of black and white stripes."

"I'd never thought of that. Which is your favorite animal at the zoo?"

"This idea of a favorite sounds strange to me," she said. Her hand touched her chain. Her mood and face changed. "I'm fond of owls."

"Owls?" Jack said. Sheldon showed interest, too.

"They see the world like we do." Her hands came to her face and she curled her fingers around her eyes. "Binocular vision. They have claws that face forward and backwards at the same time, and their heads can turn in a complete circle."

"You know a lot about owls," Jack said.

"But what I most admire about owls is they hunt between dusk and dawn. Their hearing is superb, so they can locate their prey without seeing it."

"Incredible." Jack set his fork down and used his napkin. "Any other animals?"

"Snakes."

"Snakes?"

"Odd, I know. I was reading in my history book that the Founding Fathers of your country once considered the rattlesnake for the national symbol."

Jack folded his napkin. "They had peculiar ideas back then. You must've read that Ben Franklin nominated the turkey for the job. He considered the bald eagle a bird 'of bad moral character.' I think there was talk of using a rattlesnake for a symbol, on account of the sound of its rattle. The warning sound of a rattle makes sense to me. The motto of 'Don't Tread on Me' isn't so bad either."

Tania's lips twisted in some kind of secret amusement. She faced Jack, eyes bright and glossy, "I think the snake as a symbol is perfect for the United States."

"Perfect how?" Sheldon asked.

"A snake has no arms or legs, but it can move undetected and raise itself on its own strength and, more importantly, it can assert its power without moving its body or its head. It uses instead its eyelids."

"Eyelids?" Jack said, looking at Tania to understand her.

She stared at him. Her head did not move. Her eyelids closed and opened.

Chapter Thirty-Two

J ack unfolded the small piece of paper.

His instructions were to meet the General in a café, in Spittelberg, the Red Light district. The place was a brothel and it served coffee. The menu looked respectable, even if what was not on it wasn't. Horns played, and a piano provided some spice. Conversations were low and discreet as church ladies in a storm of afternoon tea and gossip.

Jack knew of no men's quarterly with advice as to how to dress for a whorehouse. The joke throughout Europe was that Americans were as sophisticated as drinking champagne from a paper cup. Jack spotted a few drinkers around the room. The pros paced their intake to last the night to avoid the hard landing in the morning. Girls circulated the room. The white-slave trade was not so white. Jack heard a knockoff of Josephine Baker speaking French.

He thought to order some brandy for warmth. His teeth hadn't stopped chattering since he'd come in. Mother said in a letter once that the family dentist was offering a discount on the latest model of dentures with uranium so their owners could find them in the dark. Jack shivered. Vienna had become wind-across-the-Great-Lakes-Chicago cold, Badlands cold, or as he recalled from more recent memory, German winter forest cold.

Walker arrived. He looked like a man in need of a vice after he quit cigarettes.

Jack was the first to see the General. He nudged Walker. The bodyguards saw them coming and played the part from a gangster movie. They crossed their arms in front of their chests and clenched their jaws. The wall of flesh let Jack in, and shut Walker out.

The General invited Jack to sit. The General said he had ordered drinks. Jack saw no waiter. He sat and faced the room and Walker. Guards Hercules looked over his shoulder while his companion Cerberus kept Walker back.

"I heard you lost one of your comrades. My condolences."

A waiter placed two glasses and the bottle of cognac on the table.

"I lost two friends," Jack said.

The General poured two servings.

Jack proposed a toast. "To a friend and a brother in arms."

"This intrigues me, the distinction between a friend and a brother," the General said.

"Davies was my superior. I respected him. Whittaker fought alongside me. I loved him like a brother.

The General lifted his glass. "To comrades."

"Any advice on how to deal with my losses?" Jack asked.

"Only that revenge consumes the avenger."

"Have you heard anything?" Jack asked.

"I have. Friends say this Meeks is not one to be trifled with, but something tells me you know this." The General eyes indicated Walker. "I also heard that your friend over there received visitors, and they are also dead."

The music changed at the piano. Soft jazz.

"Acquainted with his visitors?" Jack asked.

"Unstable types. My men, on the other hand, are disciplined." The General took hold of the bottle. The plonk of the cork made a nice sound. The slow gurgle of the cognac was better.

"God has brought us to this fork in the road, has He not, Mr. Marshall?"

"I thought Communists didn't believe in God. I suppose there is free will after all."

"As soldiers, we forfeited free will, Mr. Marshall. We follow orders."

Jack could see the chess pieces move. He pushed on. "But as officers, we issue them."

"As long as they do not contradict policy, and here we are."

Jack had to concede the point. They were here, in a Viennese brothel.

"This Meeks, he is after something. I'm told he wants names of Nazis."

"And what do you want, General?"

"For you to realize I'm not your enemy, Mr. Marshall."

"You don't want the names of Nazis?"

"Who is to say I don't have them?"

Jack tasted the cognac. "Only way you'd know any names is, either you have a mole in my office, or..."

"What, that I took your precious typewriter ribbons?""

"Did you?" Jack asked.

The General took out a Russian cigarette, lit it, and exhaled blue smoke. "I did not take your typewriter ribbons because I don't need them."

"No Nazis for you then?" Jack asked.

"Think it through, my friend. Why would I need to steal your ribbons, when the Red Army boxed and shipped every Nazi memo to Moscow as it moved into Berlin? Surely, you know this."

"But people and papers are known to fall through the cracks, General."

"I read you were at Dachau. A question for you. You saw the Jews, yes?"

Jack could never forget the sight. When the half-dead and starved prisoners realized that the Allies had liberated the camp, they set out to kill the guards. Jack had to order his own men to stand down from shooting them, too.

"Yes, I saw them, and your point is?"

"Where were the Russians at Dachau?"

"I'm certain there were some there, why?" Jack asked.

"The Jews, the Nazis worked and gassed. They would sometimes shoot them and dump their bodies into pits, but do you know what they did to Russians prisoners of war? Rather than waste space in their gas chambers or their ammunition, they would have the prisoners run into their electrified fences around the camps. You now have your answer as to why a Nazi with information won't run to Stalin."

Jack couldn't resist. "One could say that gives you a motive to find and kill them."

"I despised the Nazi's, Mr. Marshall." He sighed. "I must admit that I rather enjoy the ironies."

"Ironies?"

"With you Americans dropping the bomb, you have created a new war."

Jack accepted the answer. "And the other irony?"

"The remaining Nazis have become Wandering Jews."

Jack drank and placed his glass on the table. "And I thought you were going to say that it's ironic that we were once allies, and now we are enemies. Bomb or no bomb, capitalism and communism are mortal enemies."

"Ideology is the long night of a dead soul, my friend."

"What can you tell me about Meeks?" Jack asked.

The General spelled out possibilities, but committed to none. Meeks was an American, and he played spy for two teams, the Americans and the British. None of this surprised Jack, until the General intimated that there were men in the upper echelons of the British government who were sympathetic to Communism.

"So Meeks has support on high, but what's his game?" Jack asked.

"He likes art and valuable things, but I suggest you to take a philosophical approach."

"I'm listening."

"Which is better, to be feared or loved?"

"Reading Machiavelli in translation these days, General? Don't tell me, you're here to tell me that love makes the world go round. You're saying Meeks is ambitious for power?"

The man smiled. "No, Mr. Marshall. Politicians have existed since the beginning of time, and I am aware that some men have no need for love. Meeks is his own man, with his own appetites. Fear might get you compliance, but love earns you loyalty and trust, which brings me back to you, Davies, and Whittaker."

"How so?" Jack asked.

"Is not your revenge predicated on loyalty and trust?"

"What would it cost me to find Meeks?"

"You think the American dollar buys you everything?"

"I wasn't thinking American money." Jack took out the Constantine.

Chapter Thirty-Three

The Den was in the basement of the old military barracks, the Stiftskaserne, in Esterhazy Park, southwest of the city center. It was a clean establishment, on the surface. Behind the nice décor, nicer lighting, and immaculate floors, the vices were as old as they were biblical. Customers had the benefit of a church nearby where they could confess their sins after the fact.

Security. There were plenty of soldiers, in need of some extra money. Hard men for the soft job of guarding entrances and exits. Dress them up in civilian clothes, turn them loose in a playground of sloppy drunks and loose women, a grunt in a suit remained a grunt, and reflexes kicked in when punches were thrown. Jack could spot a boot on patrol. A military man never lost his signature gait and posture.

Musicians in the band serenaded the crowd from behind the stand on a raised stage. Players played and probably kept a gun by their feet. Women worked the room, with that forlorn look inside of a knockout dress because men were more interested in baccarat, cards, and dice.

Jack read for character and vice. The man in glasses could pass for a scholar, but his erudition included literature best read in a lavatory. He liked wheel games. The business tycoon exuded confidence, but is a merciless tyrant who drives his wife to tears for serving his cocktail at the wrong hour, mixed wrong, in the wrong glass, and with the wrong amount of ice. He tries to sharp the cards. There's the nice guy, the guy women call at 3am when their beaus are asleep like one of the Apostles in the Garden. He plays the dice games because he hasn't a chance of luck with any of the ladies. Then

Jack spotted him, the maverick, the most dangerous gambler of all. He was the cipher, unreadable as a doctor's handwriting.

Jack picked him as his mark because the General said that he was the one to target. The maverick sat at the poker table, the second game, after politics, invented for liars.

Walker asked him from behind. "Is he the one?" Jack nodded.

A woman with enormous Crawford eyes saw Jack smile and took it as her invitation for an approach. She was holding a flute of champagne, and her hair was styled in a Victory Roll. Walker had spotted her incoming and warned Jack, "You're on your own, brother."

"Anyone ever tell you that you look like Clark Gable," she murmured to Jack.

Her eyes did the rest of the talking up and down Jack's frame.

"Good line, sister," Jack said.

"I'm not your sister, unless it's absolutely necessary." She added the flutter of eyelashes. Her hand dropped down to smooth out her dress so Jack received the newsflash that she had a body if he didn't like her for her personality.

Jack peered down his nose to meet her eyes, avoiding the deadly drop into her neckline. "That table over there, the guy there everyone seems to worship."

She looked. "What about him?"

"Happen to come across his name in your travels?"

She took a ladylike sip from her flute and looked. "That's Mr. Smith?"

"I thought Smith was a name for restaurants and hotel registers."

"Nobody here uses real names; it keeps things respectable and hard to prove in a court if the police raid the place."

"That's a shame since that means we'll never get to know each other's names."

"Oh, we don't need names for that." She set her glass down onto a passing tray and placed her hand on Jack's elbow, pulling him like he was the ship and she was his personal tugboat. Her hips rubbed against Jack's side. "See the two men behind him?"

"I saw them."

"Bodyguards. Russians, but not the kind who read Pushkin or Chekhov."

Jack could tell from their oversized jackets they were carrying, likely under both arms. The way their heads moved suggested by-the-book surveillance and crowd control, and likely, former military police, which meant they'd never seen combat outside of a disorderly drunk.

"You do all right," he said. "You know the room and I mean that as a compliment."

She squared off with Jack as if she were about to dance with him. Both of her hands took his and she pulled him closer to her. Her grip and strength surprised Jack. She looked up at him. "Move in for a kiss."

"We hardly know each other," Jack said.

"I wouldn't kiss you on the lips until we knew each other better. Do as I say."

Jack came down to her cheek, his lips about to make their mark on her, when he heard her whisper into his ear, "The General says to ask for a private game with Smith. Give the name Jones."

She pulled away. "Good luck," she said and disappeared into the crowd. Jack stood there.

"You all right?" Walker asked him, again from behind.

"That was the damndest thing."

"You know you look funny when you kiss."

* * *

Mr. Smith saw him coming. So did his hired help. Jack announced himself as Mr. Jones, and that he wished to have a private match with Mr. Smith. The dealer asked the other players to vacate the table. They were welcome to stay and watch. The dealer cleared the table and paid the dismissed players.

The General was earning his Constantine.

Smith suggested the opposite chair. Walker stood behind Jack, opposite to Smith's bodyguards. The two Russians looked sturdy, solid, and weaned on pelmeni and vodka.

The first few hands were nothing but feelers for a player's style and temperament. No bluffs. No showdowns. The stakes increased, enough to choke the race horse, but not kill it. Jack was playing with government money.

They had agreed on a variety of poker. It was poker that chased romance out the door and made showdowns a necessity. Hands came and went until Jack noticed his hands kept getting better so he wagered more aggressively. The dealer had to be on the General's payroll. The fix was in, and the con was on.

Jack as Jones taunted Smith with a grin here and there, but kept it short of contempt or arrogance. He planned to leave Smith with enough change for a taxi and a down payment on dignity. Jack announced he was tired after Smith insisted on an all-or-nothing hand to recoup his losses. The man insisted and pushed all his money forward in a sea of chips to tempt Jack.

Jack looked to the dealer. The dealer dealt.

Jack's pair of aces took the pot. Jack stood up, offered his hand out for the handshake, but Smith gave him a dirty look. Jack buttoned his jacket, gave the Russian bodyguards a wink, and waited for the dealer to count the chips and write the ticket for the trip to the Cashier's window. Jack tipped the dealer two black chips.

With the dealer's note for the Bank in his hand, Jack made his way to the window for the payout with Walker at his side. He surrendered the slip of paper to the man with the green eyeshades. Mid-way through the count, the cashier yanked down his window so hard and fats that it could have heated the glass. Jack and Walker hesitated to turn around.

Behind them was a man in a tuxedo, oiled black hair, and a pale face with a pencil-thin moustache across his upper lip in a perfect palindrome. Behind him was Mr. Smith and behind Smith, his two obedient Russians.

"Let us make this easy before the choir behind me starts singing," Smith said.

Jack pointed to the shuttered window with his thumb. "I'd like to get paid first."

"Not possible," the tuxedoed man said. "There's been an irregularity."

Jack cracked wise. "Heard prunes are good for constipation."

That was all it took. Mr. Smith lunged forward and his own mastiffs had to pull him back.

"He's a cheat, I tell you. Nobody beats me, not that fast."

The man with the Warren William moustache spoke, "Shall we adjourn to a more private room, gentlemen?"

"We shall not," Walker responded.

"It wasn't a request," the man in the tuxedo responded. He pulled out a switchblade, and everyone heard the sound of the blade sprung.

Walker unleashed a left hook that found nothing but air. One of the Russian bodyguards grabbed the tuxedoed creep's wrist and twisted it. The knife dropped. The Russian flung him into the wall. Everything about the man, including the caterpillar above his lip, lay still.

Two Russians advanced in unison. One of them came for Walker, the other took hold of Jack's shirt and steered him to the door.

* * *

When Jack came to, the back of his head ached like Lady Day's voice on the turntable. He let out a soft feminine moan no man would admit to and when he wanted to rub the sore spot he realized his hands were tied to a chair. Somebody had prepped him for the POW treatment, the same kind of Q and A Walker had received at the gasometer.

A sliver of light in the darkness indicated a door had opened, and the sounds of feet told Jack that somebody was there and this somebody knew exactly where in the room he sat. More sounds, more movements in the room.

A match was lit. Sulfur perfumed the air, as a small orange flame touched the end of a cigarette. The cigarette was a sign of civilization but Jack was confident that the owner behind the smoke was a barbarian.

It smelled of Joe, of an American brand of smokes.

The overhead light went on. It was hard to believe something so white like light could be offensive to the eyes, but it was. Jack's eyes adjusted to the glare after some blinks and squints.

An image came into focus. The smoker had rolled-up the sleeves of his shirt, the forearms were muscular, and devoid of tattoos. There was no tie, and the face was shaved, and the feet moved with a silence that suggested experience. Jack saw the mug again. The face was tough as the waterfront, the kind rats ran away from in a hurry.

"Comfortable?"

"Seen and had better," Jack replied.

"Some mess you're in here."

"And here we are, you and I, about to talk about Michelangelo," Jack said.

"Poetic. The game was rigged."

"Who said the game was fixed?" Jack asked.

"The dealer. He fessed up to the whole thing before he went for a swim."

"You don't say," Jack responded.

"Shame he knew how to swim too, so I had to let some of his air out."

The inquisitor pulled out an ice pick with a cork on one end. The stop piece prevented the owner from inadvertently stabbing himself. He unscrewed the stopper as if he were opening a bottle of wine.

"And there's a rumor you own a rare coin." The man lowered his head so his eyes met Jack's. "Your dealer couldn't swim like Davies could. He was a feisty one. He struggled until he didn't. The nice thing about an ice pick is it's nice and clean."

Jack's stomach hit the bottom of the chair. He knew how efficient an ice pick was. An ice pick bought time. Stab a man quick and fast in a crowd and he might not even know he was stuck until the killer was a city block away. The weapon was also easy to conceal and hard to defend against, too. To block the weapon assumed the victim saw the perp. Davies had seen his killer.

"Who is Davies?" Jack asked.

"No Academy Award for you. Don't worry. Davies didn't give you up, Mr. Marshall."

"What is it that you want from me?"

"A penny for your thoughts, or I should say, a Constantine," the man said.

"Is that all?"

The man eyed Jack with suspicion because Jack's answer had surprised him, since it implied that he would surrender the coin. No mess. No fuss. Experience in the field had taught Jack that torturers were not brutish men but rather astute psychologists who tested limits and fears, and they played the game of friend and enemy with a delicate blend of truths and lies.

"Time is of the essence Mr. Marshall."

"What, no sodium pentothal tonight?"

"Truth serum?"

"I've been waiting years to find out about all those lies I've been telling myself."

"Witty. I admire that. Sodium pentothal is unreliable. A better agent is ethanol."

The man's answers had confirmed Jack's guess, that the man was a professional.

"Booze is better?" Jack said.

"In its pure form, it works magnificently. Shall we start?"

He pulled up a chair and placed it in front of Jack. He placed the tip of the ice pick against Jack's shoulder. "Where is the Constantine?"

"I don't know."

The tip pushed in a little.

"Where is the Constantine?"

"Said, I don't know."

The tip touched a nerve.

"Where is the Constantine?"

"Haven't a clue," Jack answered. He knew the man could do this all night, would do it all night until his ice pick touched bone. The man retracted the pick. He held it up in front of Jack so he could see the touch of red. The man showed Jack where on the shank the ice pick would pierce bone.

"I have no personal interest in hurting you. You're an American and I'm an American."

Jack felt light as cheap cotton. The man's voice drifted off. Jack thought to conserve his strength for the next round. The man had no interest in hurting him, but he had killed Davies and the card dealer.

Jack knew torturers tried to bond with their victims. They'd talk picture shows, movie stars, or relay the latest disappointment with a sports team. They tell lies and use euphemisms. It reminded Jack of how back home the high-minded newspapers used the word 'sepia' when they meant colored folks. The reading public might call a Negro man 'boy' or worse. Jack had seen Negroes fight and die, so whenever he met a Negro on a street back home he called him Mister.

Fingers snapped in front of him. Jack's eyes flashed open.

"Pain does some remarkable things to the human mind, Mr. Marshall. First thing you do is become philosophical about life. Late in the game you become outright loony. Shall we get back to our talk?"

Before Jack had a chance to respond to the man, he had driven the ice pick deeper into his shoulder. Jack gasped, but nothing came out of his mouth. No smile, lots of teeth, and a little spit. Jack made an animal noise. He didn't remember the rest of it, except for a vague awareness of screaming, and the sound of the question.

"Where is the Constantine?" and then he said the tired phrase of every torturer, worth the head shrinker's bill, "Only you can make it stop."

Chapter Thirty-Four

When the door to the room opened, Jack stirred in the chair, his white shirt pink, his shoulder throbbed, and pain radiated down his arm. He opened his eyes and lifted the cannonball that was his head. His smile died faster than a lottery ticket one number short of the prize.

In front of him stood Meeks in a morning suit, waistcoat, blood-red cravat, tailcoat, and crimson pocket square. Jack mumbled something incoherent.

"I haven't all day, Jack," the man said, as he checked his pocket watch.

Jack's eyes focused and he responded like a drunk who glimpsed sunlight and felt the cop's less than gentle foot. "You bastard."

"Where is the Constantine?"

"Where's Joe with the ice pick?"

"Busy. The Constantine, Jack?"

"I don't get you," Jack mumbled. "Why the coin?"

Jack moved and acknowledged the pain in his shoulder.

"It's an art piece of significant cultural importance."

"Communists don't care about art."

"I'm not a communist," Meeks said. "I'm an art collector."

"And collect a Nazi for two hundred when you land on Go."

"Tell me where the Constantine is."

Jack said, "I'll tell you the same thing I told him. I don't know. Need I spell it out for you in city lights?"

"A shame. We'll find that coin, one way or another."

Jack recognized the look. He'd been at enough meetings with career officers who would look at the war dead as names on a list, names that meant a telegram, a folded flag, a note to a mother and father that their boy wasn't coming home, to a wife, no husband and to a child, no father. It was that look. Meeks had perfected it from one war to the next.

Meeks walked the walk of a warden about to tell a man that his reprieve had been denied. He whispered, "You protected the Jew, so we went after him, but he was at work so we took his girl."

Jack wanted to spit in the man's face and say something about Tania, but he didn't want Meeks to have the satisfaction, or know that he had met the girl.

Meeks hooked his thumbs into the loops of his trousers. "You can help her, Jack. Only you can save that poor girl from grief. No telling what our friend with the ice pick might do to her, and I must say she is a morsel, front and back. I'm old, but I'm not dead."

"Is this what this is all about, Meeks?"

"What are you talking about?"

"The coin."

"Tell me where it is, and everything ends here. One word, and the girl goes free."

"What does the Constantine get you, Meeks?"

Meeks considered the question. "It puts me in good with certain people."

"Art snobs, or the Russians in Moscow?"

"There are more than Russians involved, Jack."

"Oh, I forgot the British hooligans."

"They are tolerated, and I keep them content."

"Content with what?" Jack asked.

"One way or the other, I'll get the coin. Since you're of no help, I'll see what the girl knows about the coin and the Jew. Rest assured, I will find him, and learn what he knows about Nazis in Vienna."

"Nobody has proven the man knows a thing, or that has killed anyone, Meeks."

"Now who is naïve, Jack?"

"If he is a Nazi-killer, people will sympathize, but one thing people despise is a traitor."

"Rationalize all you want, Jack Marshall, but let me tell you about your murderous Jew friend. Did you know he killed the janitor in his building? He stuffed the body into a furnace in the basement. And that Russian the Jew introduced you to? He's the traitor. He led you to the Den, fronted your game of poker, and arranged for the winning cards to find their way into your hands. Think that maybe once he has the Constantine you've served his purpose? What do you say to that?"

"If you thought he had the Constantine, I wouldn't be in this chair, Meeks."

"Or maybe he and the Jew are working hand in hand."

The door opened. Meeks met with the visitor and they exchanged words.

Meeks returned to Jack and said it was time to go. The restraints loosened, Jack stood and his arm sang a song of pain. The man with Meeks was about as gentle as a veteran nurse. He jerked Jack's arm almost out of the socket. Jack reacted. "Watch it, will ya? You forget there's not enough love in the world?"

In the hallway, Jack saw Walker who, emerging from a room of his own, looked as good as he felt. Jack found comfort in seeing his old friend's face. The Russian escort with Walker had the look of a thirsty man interrupted from his drink of cold water. Jack would have kicked the cup out of his hands if he could.

Another door opened and the torturer emerged with a bloodied cheek. Tania was behind the sadist, twisting and screaming. She said some unladylike things in Russian. Meeks led the entourage down the hallway.

They crossed the emptied game room of the Den. A few sweepers were cleaning the room. They saw nothing and heard nothing. They worked their brooms across the floor, and restored chairs around the casino.

From the looks of him, the interrogator had plied his trade with some success with Tania. His zipper was undone, and his shirttails hung outside his pants. Tania looked tired, her hair stringy from sweat, one cheek bruised from a punch or a slap, but there was no sign of the ice pick used on her.

Meeks opened one last door, which opened out to a quadrangle. A sedan appeared in the distance. Another car crept behind it. Meeks had arranged for transport. All it took was a short walk across some grass. Jack and Walker bumped shoulders. Their feet stuttered to find time to read what was ahead of them and around them. Tania kept the torturer's hands full, making him regret his life's calling.

Walker looked up at the sky, unsure whether it would be his last sight of the world. It was a gray sky before it turned blue. He had had a good life. Nothing had gone as planned but it had been a good life. He saw the Flakenturm, that monstrosity Hitler had built for aerial warfare.

He also saw the silhouette of a man on the platform of the tower.

The man in dark clothes dipped down, out of sight.

Walker nudged Jack, who looked up. Meeks led. Tania screamed and scratched her guard. He pushed and pulled her, back and forth, up and down like a yo-yo as they walked across the grass.

There was a flash from the tower, followed by the sound as if the air had cracked.

Jack doubled over and reached for his ankle, his weapon out. He hit his man with the butt of his revolver, the nose now a gruesome butterfly. He rolled onto his hip in Walker's direction. Walker and his handler struggled until Jack put a bullet through the back of his head.

Jack turned prone and searched for Tania, but found that he wasn't needed. She had managed to seize the ice pick. She had straddled her man, the steel chisel in her hands. The steel glinted in the first rays of sunlight. Then came the screams. Blood spattered her face, and the golden light had transformed Tania's white blonde hair into flames of fire. She stabbed her victim again and again.

Jack and Walker looked for Meeks and found him afield.

He was dead. There was no need to look at the face because there was none.

The sniper's bullet had decapitated the southern gentlemen.

A squeal of sirens and squad of cars converged on the scene. A swarm of policemen, weapons drawn, streamed out.

It was over.

Walker turned his head to look for Tania. She remained mounted on top of the corpse. She was no girl, no outraged victim. She swung her leg over and collapsed onto her back. Walker looked the other way, exhausted.

* * *

The Inspector approached. One of his men covered Tania with a blanket. Another man offered Jack and Walker cigarettes and coffee. They accepted the beverages, refused the cigarettes.

"A fine morning, and what a mess," the Inspector said.

Jack sampled the brew, looked down at the cup. "Damn good coffee, Inspector."

"Glad you approve," the man said, his hands behind his back. His eyes surveying the field. He noticed the tower. "Towers seem to be a recurring theme with us. Was the shooter one of your men?" Jack shook his head. "Care to explain how all of you arrived here?"

Jack finished his coffee. "Not really."

"I see. If I were one to conjecture something drew you to an alleged gambling establishment nearby. What do you say to that, Mr. Marshall?"

"I heard rumors are good for the local economy."

The Inspector looked in the direction of the dead Meeks.

"The dead man over there. Is he somehow tied to the murder in the sewer?"

"Sounds reasonable to me, Inspector."

"And the man over there with that ghastly thing in his face?"

"What about him?" Jack said.

"Confident the same ice pick was used on the late Davies?"

"Confident, yes, and I'm certain it can be connected to another crime."

"What other crime?"

"You might find a young man in the sewers. He worked at the gambling establishment you mentioned. Those men in that car over there, Inspector. Who are they?"

"Art students, I believe. I can provide you with a copy of the report."

"You can do that?" Jack asked.

The Inspector shrugged. "Papers are known to fly in the wind."

"I wouldn't mind seeing the records on those art students, particularly their visas. I'd like to know where else they studied." Jack's eyes looked toward Meeks. "And, I wouldn't mind seeing a ballistics report."

Chapter Thirty-Five

The German equivalent of OFFICIAL COPY was stamped on the bottom of the ballistics report. It was a one-pager in dense German prose. The attention to detail would have made the IRS envious. Jack poured himself a whiskey for company.

There were no footprints or fingerprints. Nothing. The rifle had been dusted for prints and for the telltale cheek smudge. Zilch. The 7.62mm self-loading sniper rifle was textbook Tokarev and capable of twenty-five to forty shots per minute. The telescopic sight made the rifle accurate up to six-hundred meters. This rifle was not as good as the Mosin-Nagant used to kill the Nazi in the city square from the earlier report.

Jack's mouth enjoyed the way the whiskey grabbed his taste buds and stung his tongue.

What pleased him most in the report was this sentence:

'This rifle will produce muzzle fire that can/will betray the sniper's position.'

Walker entered the room. "I haven't seen that smile in a long time."

Jack found a clean glass for Walker, and poured his friend some. Walker took his glass and enjoyed the aroma first, and accepted the paper from Jack. "Ballistics report?"

"Straight from the Inspector's desk," Jack said.

Walker skimmed the page. "Reader's Digest version, please."

"Says the shooter picked a rifle known for muzzle fire."

"Odd that a sniper would pick a weapon that would betray his position, don't you think?"

Jack said, "I think it was deliberate, but it does apply pressure to make the shot count."

"Sounds confident about his skills if you ask me," Walker said.

"He wanted us to see him, and that's not the only thing he did that was intentional." Jack held up a photograph of the rifle. Walker squinted. Jack turned the photo around for him to review it again. Walker said, "It's a different rifle."

"It's Soviet, like the Mosin-Nagant, except this one is a Tokarev." Jack looked at Walker, like a teacher expecting the correct answer from his prized pupil. "See the implication?"

Walker answered, "Two Russian rifles make it look like a Soviet sniper did the work."

"And the story here writes itself," Jack said. "The folks back home will think Reds wanted Meeks dead. With their lead dog put down, they'll appoint someone else to replace him, keep him stateside for safety reasons, and they'll throw more money at the Company because the Kremlin has assassins in the field."

"Meeks is a martyr for the cause, there's no interest in Sheldon as a suspect, and it's a victory lap for us."

"Exactly," Jack said. "Sheldon is a clever one."

Walker placed his glass on the desk. Jack picked up the bottle, but Walker said no. The whiskey went to sleep in the desk drawer.

"And those art students. Anything on them?" Walker asked.

"Hodge-podge of anti-socials, intellectuals, and world-on-fire idealists."

"And our friend with the ice pick?"

"Served as an MP, but nothing more, which troubles me, Walker. A torturer learns his trade somewhere and from someone."

"Think he was like Leslie, British but passed for American?"

"I doubt it," Jack asked.

"Why not?" Walker said.

"I'm thinking mercenary. Like Meeks and Whittaker, everyone has something on the side these days. Speaking of torture, how is Tania?"

"Leslie tried talking to her, woman to woman, but Tania is keeping her emotions tight to the vest. I imagine it all takes time."

"Women are stronger than us when it comes to trauma," Jack said. "Children, in particular, are resilient, but there's always that chance the wiring short-circuits later."

"What do we do with Sheldon?"

"I had files of Nazis, who were of no use to us, delivered to him. It'll look like we gave him something without compromising ourselves."

"Generous of you, but that's not what I meant, Jack."

"I'm working with the Inspector on exit papers for the two of them. Was that your question, or was something else on your mind?"

"When we brought Tania to his place, he asked me to give you something." Walker reached into his pocket and held it up for Jack to see the Constantine.

"I didn't expect to see this again," Jack said, accepting the rare coin.

Walker rose from his seat. "On that note, I am off."

"Plans?"

"Dinner with Leslie."

"You two an item now? I heard a rumor that she is leaving MI6."

Walker stood there. "Speaking of rumors, I heard the office is moving to Munich."

"Interested?" Jack asked.

"Haven't a clue. Give me a crumb as to the mission there."

"Making sure the Company's man there has what he needs."

Chapter Thirty-Six

"Alles schläft, einsam wacht," Walker hummed and sang to the man in the mirror as he looped and adjusted the knot in his tie. All was calm, all was bright, to paraphrase the Christmas song. Walker had achieved the impossible. He dreamt in German and his conversations with the locals had improved somewhat. Even his choice of tie was an accomplishment. He had trained his eye in colors, in combinations and patterns. His neckties were no longer humdrum, nor did they broadcast his presence like the RKO Radio Picture tower either. He slipped on his latest suit jacket, Ulster overcoat, and adjusted the lapels. He checked his reflection, his profile. Walker looked and felt like Fifth Avenue.

Leslie had picked the restaurant, a French place in the First District. Any eatery in the vicinity of City Hall, the theatre district, and the university saw its share of bureaucrats, intellectuals, and thespians for clientele. The Viennese threw around titles and honorifics the way folks back home fed change into parking meters. With the right customers and the right amount of Austrian deference, the successful French restaurateur and his chef de cuisine could park a von in front of their last name.

A breeze filled with some rain swept down Lichtenfelsgasse. Leslie was quick with a gloved hand to her head to save her hat. Walker reached for his fedora in time. The tempest didn't prevent them for dressing up for a night on the town. In a black cocktail dress, with some sparkles around her throat, a fur stole and shawl that matched the ensemble, Leslie capped off the show with legs in peep-toe heels. Walker saw the bullet-shaped bodice as a concealed weapon he'd love to disarm later that evening.

Her hand pulled him to a window display. "We've got time to spare," she said.

They both gawked at the great figure of a knight in a suit of armor, his visor down and both hands holding a sword. Taller than the average man, this ancestor of the American football player, he had armored plates to protect the mobile or vulnerable joints of elbows, knees, and shoulders. A part of his helmet acted as chinstrap and covered his throat. Exposure to the elements had reduced his armor to the dull shade of graphite found in a pencil. There was plaque above the statue. "Practice your German, Walker. What does it say?"

"Nagelmänner, or iron man."

Leslie knocked his shoulder with a soft punch. "C'mon, there's more to it than that."

He read the German first, and then rendered an approximate translation, all in a solemn voice. "This iron man of Vienna is a reminder of a time when suffering from war was as endless as love and charity."

Leslie pointed to a smaller sign. "Says here that people would donate money for a nail so they could hammer it into the wooden statue." Her hand grazed over a studded leg. "They did it to benefit the veterans of The Great War and their families. Apparently, the greater the donation, the bigger the nail and the donor's choice of location."

"Imagine that," Walker said. "From wood to iron man, in one generation. I imagine the rampant inflation after World War I put a little extra oomph behind the hammer they used. Says this idea for fundraising, these nail men, started in Vienna and spread throughout Austria and Germany. Have you had enough or should I hire a tour guide?"

"Let's eat," she said.

* * *

He held the door to the restaurant open for her. She coasted into a Gallic winter wonderland. The tablecloths were white as snow. Slim Frenchmen in pressed uniforms cute as arctic hares hustled around the room. Midway to their table with the maître d,' they stopped to allow an express train of cloches on silver trays on shoulders.

A waiter pushed in the chair behind Leslie.

They read the menu to decide on their courses. Their small talk was in German, talk with the water boy and waiter, in French. The restaurant was like theatre, in that they didn't talk to be overheard. Parisian French, to use Leslie's word, sounded posh. It didn't help Walker that what little French he remembered from the classroom was nothing like the French he heard in the streets or in the field as a soldier.

Not a word English was heard in the place.

* * *

After dinner, they decided to walk off their meal. Leslie carried a small box of pastries in one hand, her other hand held Walker's arm. The bright moon knocked out the stars. A car wheezed by, the sound of a diesel engine. Walker could hear her questions before they reached the taxi stand. His answers would determine whether he went home with her, or home alone.

"Where do you see yourself in five years?" she asked.

"Five years seems far away. I mean, I know it isn't, but the war lasted six years, and that felt like a lifetime to me."

"Time waits for no one," she said.

"Assessing my ambition?"

She looked at him and smiled. "Don't think I am sizing you up as a prospective mate. It's a simple question, and only that."

"And you want an answer?"

"I wouldn't have asked, if I didn't. Say what you will, and don't apologize for what you think and feel."

"No apologies, huh? Sounds dangerous," he said, and their eyes met.

"This isn't a trick question, Walker."

"I suppose I can revise whatever I say."

"Revision suggests a lack of conviction."

He whistled. "You sound like Jack."

"Then don't revise, Walker. State the truth."

"The truth is what we tell ourselves. Jack's words."

She pulled on his arm. "No quotes, no evasive maneuvers, please."

"You want the truth? Why don't you start?"

"So you can paraphrase what I say so I think we're simpatico?"

"A guy can try, can't he?" Walker said.

"It'll take more than that to get into my bed."

"Wow," he said. "You're direct, straight for the throat."

"You want to hear the truth?" She relaxed her grip. "The truth is women have to apologize all the time to men because if they don't they are either a threat, or considered unladylike. How am I doing so far?"

"I'm not most men, and if I were, you wouldn't be here with me."

He had put some points on the board, or so it seemed, because she smiled.

"Clever response," she said. "You say you are different than most men."

"You say that as if you don't believe me."

"Time will tell," she said. "Where do you see yourself in two years?"

"I am not sure, and that's an honest answer."

"See yourself as a Company man?"

"As opposed to what?"

"You tell me." Her voice seemed casual, but he sensed a strategy in play. An open-ended question was conducive to communication, but here, it was as if each word in his answer was to be weighed for confidence, for hesitation, and for sincerity. He repeated himself, "As opposed to what, Leslie?"

The moonlight liked her face. "There's a thing called free will. Heard of it?"

"I have. I could try the GI Bill again, but I don't have a mind for business. I don't see myself as a bean counter for the rest of my life."

"But can you see yourself as an insurance man for Jack?"

"He offered a solution, an easy answer. I'm not ashamed to say it, Leslie."

"But you have to decide whether it's a temporary or not. This life doesn't get any easier. The longer you stay in this line of work, the harder it becomes, Walker. Is that you want?"

Walker could've imitated Jimmy Stewart's aw-shucks demeanor but he didn't. She was earnest and serious, and she deserved an honest answer. He told her, "I do have another idea, with the GI Bill, but I don't think I could pull it off."

She tugged on his arm. "What's this idea?"

"You'd laugh if I told you."

"I won't laugh, I promise. Tell me."

"Writing. I always wanted to be a writer. And we both know how that pays the bills."

"Is a lack of confidence what stops you?"

"That, and the feeling that I have nothing to say because I haven't lived life. Ironic, isn't it? I've lived a life that I can't talk about."

"Plenty of writers in our line of work. You know that, right?"

"I could use a pseudonym, I suppose. Any other questions?"

"What's the hardest part of the job for you?"

Her eyes looked into his, and they almost unnerved him. Almost.

"If I answer that question, Leslie, you have to answer it, too."

"I will if you will."

He had enough experience now, from wearing a military uniform to a suit for the Company that she was asking one of two questions. The easier question was how he lived with violence if the job demanded it. The vast majority of Company personnel never had to resort to it, like most police officers never drew their weapon on the beat. The second question was harder, more realistic, so he would give her an answer to that one without any need for revision.

"The hardest part is living the lie, living the double life. Take Jack, for example."

Her face flashed surprise. "What about him?"

"He is married, and he doesn't talk to his wife about his work."

"How do you know he doesn't?"

"Because I know Jack. As far as the world is concerned, Jack Marshall is an insurance man, nine to five, fifty weeks a year minus the two weeks for vacation that isn't a vacation because the clock never sleeps. What about you?"

"What about me?"

"I'll make it easier for you, and lob the same softball question you first put over the plate. Where do you see yourself in two years?"

"Men and their sports analogies," she said. "I'll tell you where I don't see myself."

"I'm listening, and I won't judge."

"We always judge, Walker. It's how people stay alive."

"I said I'd listen. Swing at the ball, or it's a strike."

"American or British, the choices for a woman are nurse, secretary, teacher, or wife. I don't see myself as any of the above. How's that sound?"

Walker said, "None of the above, huh? The experience with the tea tray is proof that you're not suited for the secretarial arts, which leaves us with teacher. Any chance there?"

"Teach women in intelligence? I doubt I'd get past the Boys Club within MI5 or MI6."

"And life as a wife?"

"Doubt it," she said.

"Thought so. I don't see you, martini in hand for hubby home from work, pies on the windowsill, and a house all spick and span. Nope, no picket fence for Leslie, and forget about sex once a week, always in the missionary position. Accurate so far?"

Leslie was silent for a moment. "Only once a week? How sad. Quite the dreary picture you've painted, Walker. Is there any light in this portrait?"

"Stay with us, stay with the Company."

"Tempting," she said.

"Which brings us to the question about the hardest part of the job."

She stopped and faced him. "You could walk away, and become that writer."

"You can, too. Walk away, I mean."

"You've forgotten the first lesson of the job," she said.

"Remind me, because I'm learning as I go."

"Rules one and two are observe and listen. Those two are interchangeable, and the third rule is, do your best not to draw attention to yourself."

"But your advice is, get out while I can?"

"Correct."

"Avoid the double life, huh?"

"Step away, while you can," she said. "The energy to maintain the lie disappears. You can put it all inside a box, like you did with your medals, with the awful memories you have of the war, and forget everything. Start fresh, start anew. Reinvent yourself."

"Something tells me you're going to say none of that applies to you."

"Neither nurse, secretary, teacher, nor wife be I," she said.

"And what if I said, you're not most women? You could do whatever you want."

"It's a sweet compliment, thank you, but an illusion."

"Why not? You don't have to stay with the Company."

"It suits me, Walker."

"Living the double wife suits you?"

"Men don't realize no woman is accepted as she is. We already live a double life."

"Because you're a woman?"

"Yes. Let me ask you a question, Walker. When you enter a room, what is the first thing you do? The very first thing, answer without thinking."

"I determine entrances and exits, and I size up any potential threats in a room. Why?"

"A girl learns that instinctively by the time she learns how to put on her first brassiere. There's also another crucial difference. Give or take the circumstances, a man is armed. Women are not, so we are left to our own devices."

Walker shook his head. "Life is unfair is what you're saying, so let me ask you this: what is the first thing you do when you enter a room? Answer without thinking."

She stared at him for a second. "Entrances and exits, size up the territory, and look for the nearest thing I can use as a weapon."

"Even if you're armed?"

"Men don't respect boundaries, and often think either I don't know how to handle a weapon, or that I'll use it."

"What are you saying, Leslie?"

"Society has women change masks for every occasion, which is why women make for better spies."

"Except you've forgotten one thing, Leslie."

"Have I?"

"We all wear masks."

"Intelligence is the one field where a woman can use her mind, her body, and on occasion, both. It may all seem like acting, but she writes the script."

He nodded. "So living the lie comes naturally because it's the norm for women?"

She hooked her arm around his. "You know, I was thinking of our Iron Man back there and what you said earlier."

"Oh, what did I say earlier?"

Leslie answered, "You said 'life as a wife' and a house 'spick and span.'"

"I remember."

"The spelling is different, but did you know spik is Old Norse for a nail?"

She stopped. She faced him again. He thought they might kiss. Walker's heartbeat slowed down. He had trained it to do that. He had to. Face an opponent with a hammering heart and he'd miss the shot. She surprised him and stepped away from him, arm raised. A cab pulled up. The sound of the brakes matched his anxiety. She opened the door instead of him. "The sooner you get in, the sooner we get to my place."

* * *

The next morning he rolled onto his back. He looked to the left at the nightstand. Like him, she kept a pistol there. He turned his head the other way and saw her dress draped over the phone. He could see his holster hanging over a chair. Next to Grable were her undergarments. He looked down and could see his shoes, and her heels had been kicked off and scattered in their passionate upright crawl and grope towards the bed.

His hand reached out. Her side of the bed was already cold, and the sheets were flopped over. His toes wiggled. A breeze wafted from over his toes.

The movement in the room was her, moving back and forth from armoire to vanity, clothes picked out for the day. His eyes focused.

He heard, "Coffee is on the table."

He must have fallen asleep again. He propped himself, on his elbows and back against the headboard. He viewed the field and saw that their passion had rearranged the furniture.

"About last night?" he asked.

"It was great. You were great."

He ignored the performance review and reached for the morning brew, took the lid off and took a whiff before he tasted the dark stuff. High octane. He watched her. She already had her slip on and her hair done. He searched for a clock, found none, and then realized he had misplaced his wristwatch somewhere.

"You should get dressed."

"You seem to be dressing fast enough for the both of us."

He threw a leg over to the side, then gathered up his clothes. He chose a chair to put his socks on, one foot at a time.

"I'm sorry to put you out," she said. "I'm meeting someone this morning."

"Do what you need to do. I'll be out of your way soon." He found one shoe, looked for the other. "For the record, I enjoyed myself last night."

"Glad," she said. She was at the mirror of her vanity putting on her eye shadow.

He thought he'd pass the time and offer some small talk.

"Jack says Munich is next. How do you feel about Oktoberfest?"

"I'm not going." She twisted around in her chair. He had his pants on and he was tying the laces on his other shoe. "Jack offered me something else."

"It wouldn't be the first time Jack left me out of the conversation." He found his shirt and put his arms into the sleeves. "May I ask what his offer was?"

She had her back to him. He could see her face in the mirror. He was buttoning his shirt. He had forgotten all about his coffee.

"Job in the States," she said.

"Company?"

"Yes, but it's not guaranteed."

"Why not?" he asked. "Jack's name carries weight."

"Says I have to interview with someone named Mr. Smith." She checked her eyelashes. "You'd think Jack could have come up with a more creative name than Smith."

"Smith is his real name," he told her. "His nickname is Beetle, but don't call him that. He and Jack have history. Bedell Smith is Eisenhower's right-hand man."

She turned in the chair, surprised.

He nodded. "He's ambassador to the Soviet Union at the moment, but word is he's being slotted to take over the Company. I wouldn't worry yourself too much about Beetle. Jack thinks highly of you, and that's all that matters. There will, however, be other interviews, and those you have to worry about."

"Jack mentioned Dulles."

"Did he say whether it was Allen or John?"

"He didn't say," she said, between dashes of lipstick.

"Probably Allen," Walker said as he strapped on his holster and Grable. "Allen was stationed here in Vienna once. I'd watch myself with him."

"They're brothers, right?"

"Like Frank and Jesse James."

After his wristwatch, the last thing was his coat.

She got up. She reached down to the floor. "Your hat."

"Thanks. Interested in dinner tonight?"

"Walker, I don't think that's a good idea."

"Why not?"

"We'll be working together in the States."

"Don't assume," he said. "Remember our conversation last night?"

"You were serious?"

"I was, but I guess you weren't."

"Munich is a way-station, whether you stay with the Company or not. Jack will explain it to you."

"Did Jack say anything else I should know? Scratch that," he said.

"Please don't make this difficult. It's for the best. We need to be professional."

He opened the door and stood in the hallway. She leaned against the opened door.

"I should get breakfast," he said.

Her hand disappeared out of view. She held out a box of pastries. He stared at it.

She shook the box. He looked at it, looked at her, shook his head, then turned and walked away. He wasn't the only man in Vienna to have a nail driven into him.

Chapter Thirty-Seven

Two years later. 1950

The letter was postmarked Boston, the message simple and direct, like the author's handwriting. It was an invitation to Malibu, California. He read it on his balcony that looked out over the garment district, the Buenos Aires neighborhood of Once. He set it aside and gave the invite thought. His hands gripped the railing. He watched a shooting star flash across a sky. His desire to find the monster in the maze of houses below had come to a standstill.

He phoned his landlady to tell her he would be away for a few days.

In his travel bag he placed several dress shirts, some slacks, some ties, a SIG Sauer pistol, and an underarm holster.

* * *

Sheldon arrived with the Santa Ana winds. He rented a room in downtown. He leased a car. He avoided all the flytraps set for tourists, except one, because he'd seen it in several film noir movies. He visited Angel's Flight to watch the funicular railway cars. Otherwise, he ignored the stables of mythology, the movie studios, and instead drove and drove through the new frontier of suburbs and side streets.

Los Angeles had started as an unimpressive orange grove until an aqueduct turned it into an oasis and metropolis. The glitter of lights at night said all he needed to know about the pueblo city. It was beautiful at night and unrecognizable and garish during the day. The hills were brown all the time and a dust and dryness contaminated everything. Concrete arteries clotted the landscape, diamond bridges folded over little rivers, tunnels tore into hills, and on-ramps and off-ramps kept the promise that ten minutes on a map was a half-hour in the car.

On the Arroyo Seco Parkway, after the hideous interchange, he drove from Elysian Heights through the tunnels into Pasadena, where the eucalyptus trees lined the boulevards, pungent and ready to explode in the heat. After lunch he returned to his room.

There was a dirtiness downtown, beneath the hills, away from the wealthy and their large blue-water pools. He observed the crowd and vendors. There was the prowl of rolled-up pant legs, dirty fingernails testing fruit or swatting away flies. There were boxes on cracked sidewalks under corrugated frontages. And there was the parade of porkpie hats, cheap suits and cigarettes, hard faces and soft minds, fast eyes, old eyes, tired eyes, and hawkers yelling out headlines.

Over at Fairfax, he saw Jews in flatbeds, and itinerant Mexicans in search of a day's work and wage. He saw a Negro, his eyes over the shoulder, working wherever he could, working and living where he saw more whites than they did of him. The police wore one color and saw one color.

Everyone slept under the bluest of skies that gave no thought to clouds. The chaparral dying, everything was tough. There was a veneer of meanness, an amnesia to it all. Nobody, including the sky, had time to cry, and when they did, they forgot why they did.

After a quick stroll through the haberdashery at Oviatt and Alexander's, Sheldon decided enough was enough and that it was time to call on the address. He put the suitcase in the car.

As he drove up Roosevelt Highway, a large cloud shaped like a horse raced his Chrysler. A breeze whooshed in as a continuous stream down the left side of the car and on the right, sage and brush undulated in a blur of browns and some green. Seagulls wheeled and cried in the air.

He turned right from a smooth road onto biting gravel. The car waded and wobbled down the pathway. Stones stung the car's underbelly. The note had told him to turn when he saw a post. He did. A modest incline challenged him before he entered a driveway.

He saw the four-door Kaiser Virginian on Kelsey-Hayes chrome spoke wheels with extra-wide white walls on his left. He parked and stopped to admire the Virginian before he took out two giftbags from the trunk.

Sheldon knew a thing or two about automobiles from magazines. He noted the clamshell doors. He pressed his face to the glass on the passenger side to admire the Imperial Crush floor, Stockholm and Volta cloth interior. He stepped back to appreciate the body in two-tone Onyx and Pasadena Yellow paint.

"She's a beauty, isn't she?" Walker said, as he approached Sheldon. Walker sported a new look since they'd last seen each other in Vienna. White shirt, khaki slacks, and the shirt with the top button undone. "Like the new threads?" Walker asked.

"Casual American suits you."

"Hope you didn't mind my having Tania send the invitation."

"I'm hard to reach," Sheldon said.

"I understand. The important thing is you're here. She's here, you know, and I should tell you that she's received excellent grades this semester. She was telling us she wishes to attend Smith."

"Us?"

"Jack and his family are here."

"How does she look?"

"Decide for yourself when you see her. Be happy there are no boys at Smith."

"Nice car, by the way."

"Glad you like it. The paint job is one of a kind."

Sheldon followed Walker into the house, but not before stealing one last look at the automobile. Walker held the screen door open for him. Sheldon heard the sound of heels first and then saw her. "Sheldon, how wonderful it is to see you."

"Happy to see you again, Leslie."

She hugged him and accepted his gift of Venetian glasswork.

Leslie said, "Let me take that." She meant his other bag with the large box in it.

"Your jacket, Sheldon," Walker said.

"I'll take care of it," Leslie said to Walker. "I'd like a moment with Sheldon. Betty might need some help in the kitchen. You don't mind, do you?"

"No problem. See you soon, Sheldon," Walker said.

Without saying a word, Sheldon undid the harness and handed it and the P210 inside it to Leslie, who hung the rig on a hook inside the utility closet under the stairs. She draped one of Walker's coats over it. Sheldon asked her to place his other bag underneath it.

"You said you wanted a word."

"It's about Tania."

"I hope she wasn't much trouble."

"Trouble isn't the word I would use, Sheldon." She took his arm, stood close enough to speak in a low enough voice. "Tania is quite the young lady, Sheldon, and she knows it." Leslie's voice was concerned, and her grip on his arm that of an intimate friend. "I think it might be a good idea for her to talk to someone."

"If you mean another woman, then by all means."

"As in someone professional, Sheldon."

"Professional, as in a headshrinker?"

"I didn't mean to alarm you, but I think she should talk to an analyst."

"Has she done something disconcerting?"

"Let's just say her behavior around men is precocious."

Leslie fixed his pocket square. Sheldon didn't know what to say. There was the sound of another woman calling Leslie. Before she disappeared, Leslie reminded them to go into the living room where she would bring in some iced tea. A breeze made the screen door flutter against the doorframe.

* * *

Sheldon had sat down in the parlor with Walker when he felt a herd of footsteps through the floorboards. "Daddy . . . Daddy," a little boy's and a girl's voice shouted in unison. The children entered the room and became silent when they saw him.

"Jack's kids," Walker announced.

The little boy stepped up and put out his little hand to Sheldon. "I'm John Marshall, but my friends call me Jack. Nice to meet your acquaintance and what is your name?"

"My name is Sheldon. Nice to make your acquaintance. That's a nice firm handshake, you have there." The little boy laughed when Sheldon pumped his hand up and down vigorously. He turned his attention to the small girl there, standing shy and unsure.

"And what is your name, miss?"

"Elizabeth, and not Liz or Lizzie."

"Nice to meet you Elizabeth, not Liz or Lizzie."

The girl sauntered off to join her brother, leaving Sheldon and Walker alone.

Walker said, "Before he joined the Company, Jack resumed his courtship with a woman. A buddy of his was seeing her before he shipped out for Europe. Jack's friend was killed in action. She found out she was pregnant with twins and raised the children on her own. When Jack returned from Munich, they married, and he adopted her children. The boy was already named John."

Leslie stepped in and offered iced tea. When they stood next to each other, Sheldon asked, "And what are you two up to these days?"

Walker said, "I work for Boeing. Engineering."

Leslie said, "And I thought he wanted to be a writer, but he managed to get a grant to study German at Monterey. You know how self-conscious Walker is about his German."

"Really?" Sheldon said. "German at the Institute of International Studies?"

"It was a hard sell since Arabic languages are in demand," Walker said.

"And you, Leslie, what about you?"

"I work here, in Los Angeles, doing research and analysis."

Walker said, "After Munich, of course."

"Of course, and Jack?" Sheldon asked.

"Iran and Afghanistan. The Russians are interested in the Pashtunistan area."

"Yes, the Durand Line," Sheldon said. "A different name but the same game."

The door opened and smacked wood again. A voice boomed out. It was Jack summoning the children. Footsteps stampeded. A woman's voice rang out. "What did I tell you about running in the house?"

Jack came into the parlor. He was wearing a suit Sheldon had tailored for him in Vienna. Jack held a wooden crate of fruit in his hands. Walker relieved him of it and took it into the kitchen.

An elegant woman appeared behind Jack in an apron. Jack introduced her as Betty. She apologized for not having greeted him earlier.

When the room went silent, Sheldon looked to the front door. Tania stood there, holding a small purse in her hands, in a tangerine dress tied off around the waist in black. Walker had been right. She was fifteen and already a stunner. Her hair was long and combed back. Platinum. He thought of Leslie's advice.

Sheldon walked over. Tania hugged him, held him tight, and he felt something wet on the side of his face but she wiped it away before he could see it. They sat down at the sofa.

She talked to Sheldon in a low voice, sometimes in German and sometimes in Russian, depending on the endearments. She told them she was doing well in school and she appreciated his arranging her stay with his old friend. She retrieved a small photograph of her and his friend, taken of them together in Boston.

Little Jack was playing a game of cowboys and invisible Indians with Elizabeth. She was the daughter of the U.S. Cavalry captain he had to rescue, when Leslie announced that everyone should come to the table.

This was Sheldon's first Grace. He followed Betty's lead and bowed his head. He reflected on the words he was hearing, and there was nothing there he would disagree with.

Walker carved and served the roast. Leslie tendered the side dishes. Betty checked on the children's drinks. Sheldon had pulled up his sleeves. He stopped to look around. He enjoyed this sight of a family gathered around a table, something he had long forgotten. He was listening to the sounds of cutlery when little Jack said, "Are you a good man?"

"Why do you ask?"

"Because of those numbers on your arm. Were you in prison?"

"In a manner of speaking, but it wasn't a prison like you have in America."

"So there was no barbed wire fences?"

"No, we had them."

"Guards?"

"Of course, every prison has guards and prisoners."

"What did you do?"

"Jack Marshall, Junior, change the subject." Betty said it in a tight voice.

"It's okay, Mrs. Marshall." Sheldon said to the boy, "I didn't do anything."

"But why would someone put you in prison?"

"Because it was wartime, and because some people don't like other people."

"Why?"

"Because people are different."

"Why?" the boy asked again.

His mother gave him a hard stare he ignored.

Sheldon said, "People are frightened of those who are different from them."

"That's dumb. Nobody goes to prison unless they broke the law."

Elizabeth watched in awe and curiosity, holding a piece of bread, the small half-moon bite marks around the outer edges, and her lips shiny with butter. She asked, "But doesn't that make the people who put you in prison bad?"

"Not all of them were bad, Elizabeth. Some thought they were doing the right thing."

"My daddy says people can be both good and bad. Do you agree?"

"I am not one to argue with your father." Sheldon said and smiled.

* * *

They ate until it came time to clear the dishes. Leslie and Tania helped Betty.

Walker, as the host, asked Jack and Sheldon if they wanted drinks.

Walker's study downstairs was a masculine room. The room offered two wide burgundy leather armchairs on a large area rug that seemed in permanent conversation with a fireplace. The late afternoon hour delivered a chill in the air. Jack lit a fire.

A fog soon drifted in. Sheldon was quick to learn that cold was a subjective term amongst Californians. The fire crackled and sputtered flames.

Sheldon and Walker took to the leather chairs while Jack pulled up a chair from the desk where two telephones in two different colors sat, after he had poured some whiskey. Jack added two drops of spring water to each serving before he handed them to Sheldon and Walker. He said it made this particular spirit sing. Walker sat silent in his own house. He looked into his whiskey.

"Buenos Aires is a long way from Vienna for a tailor," Jack said.

"You're in the assurance business, and Walker has become an engineer."

"One never leaves the assurance business," Jack said.

"How was Munich?" Sheldon asked.

Jack explained that Nazis who had knowledge in germ, missile, and rocket warfare were processed through Munich and relocated to various U.S. Army bases. He added that the U.S. had firmed up its commitment with the new German government and its new intelligence agency, the BND.

"You have to appreciate the irony," Sheldon said.

"What irony is that?" Jack asked.

"Davies in Vienna was a major general, and Reinhard Gehlen of the BND was a major general in the Wehrmacht." Sheldon finished his glass. Jack offered another and Sheldon accepted. "The Russians are expanding," Jack said, as he poured.

"Into Iran and Afghanistan, I heard."

"That reminds me. I have something to show you." Jack went over to the desk and opened up Walker's desk drawer. The fireplace crackled. Jack had located a nice-size envelope. He placed it on Sheldon's lap.

"What is this?"

Walker answered for Jack. "Papers inside a safe-deposit box at the Erste

Bank."

Sheldon read some of the pages. He saw names, pictures, photographs, and indecipherable numbers and letters. He said nothing.

"Your Russian general was very generous," Jack said. "Please keep reading."

Sheldon moved through the pages. He saw an unfamiliar face. He held up the photo.

Jack said, "That's the fellow Meeks was working for. He's none other than the king's art historian. His joy in life is some French painter named Poussin."

"You caught yourself a big fish," Sheldon said. "What did you do with him?"

"Threw him back into the water," Walker said.

Sheldon's forehead creased. "Why?"

Jack answered. "Nobody is interested in him. Art is not the same thing as atomic secrets."

"And you are telling me this why?" Sheldon asked.

"Because some people serve a purpose."

Walker asked, "What I don't understand is why did the Russian general help us, Jack?"

"Ambivalence about atomic weapons? A lack of options after Kursk had put him in the outhouse." Sheldon's face turned pale. Jack noticed and said, "Did I say something?"

"The General was never at Kursk."

'He wasn't?"

"No, he was a GRU officer."

"Counter-intelligence?" Jack said, nodded in acceptance. "How did you come by him then?"

"In trying to help Tania, I asked around. Like Tania's father, the general wanted to avoid the gulag."

Jack absorbed the revelation. "I was played like a record?"

Sheldon stood up. "I almost forgot. I brought you a gift. It's upstairs."

Sheldon left the room to retrieve the box in the closet. He returned and placed it on Jack's lap. Jack worked the tape off the four ends and shimmied the box. He tipped the lid loose and saw the contents before Walker did. Jack tilted the box enough for Walker to see inside. Neatly arranged in two rows, were typewriter ribbon spools.

"Meeks was right?" Jack said.

Sheldon asked, "Right about what?"

"That you took them?" Walker said.

Jack examined individual twin spools. "You knew the Nazis we had the whole time."

"I was after one, in particular," Sheldon said.

Jack looked up. "South America?"

Before Sheldon answered, Walker said, "That might explain these."

Walker crossed the room to his desk, where he opened the middle drawer and retrieved some papers. Holding them, he said, "These are reports on Nazis found shot." Walker held up a piece of paper. "You might find this interesting."

Sheldon accepted the paper, read the contents, and handed it back to Walker.

Jack said, "All of them were killed with a SIG P210. All Company weapons have a ballistic profile on record, so you can imagine my surprise when I'm in Baghdad and this report shows up. It's the pistol I gave you in Vienna."

"And in a holster upstairs," Sheldon replied and raised his glass. "Bravo, Jack Marshall, you found a clever way of keeping a line on me."

"Some fish you keep, some you release."

"You stole the ribbons for one name?" Walker asked.

"Otto Eckmann. Not his real name, of course," Sheldon answered. Walker looked to Jack for an explanation and received it. "Escaped Allied custody in '46 and obtained a permit to Argentina in '48." Jack turned his attention to their guest. "Careful with Eckmann, Sheldon."

"Because the man once worked with Gehlen?"

"Because bad things happen to good men."

A woman's voice yelled down to them that dessert was ready.

* * *

After dessert everyone visited the rec room downstairs. There was laughter and there was talk. The Marshall children played until they had tired themselves out. Outside, the winds blew and the trees swayed.

The radio on, everyone listened to a response to an alarming accusation made days earlier by a junior senator from Wisconsin. Tania sat close to Sheldon. He kissed her lightly on the temple. He looked outside at the paradise that reminded him of the Mediterranean. Palm trees swayed. There was a hint of clouds, a bright moon, and there were shadows.

Afterword

Reality is stranger than fiction is a paraphrase of a quote attributed to Mark Twain.

Not far from the White House, in Boxes 1-186 located at 230/86/46/5 within the National Archives, there are case files, dated 1945-1958, which contain dossiers on more than 1,500 German scientists. With Berlin in ruins, the United States transitioned from one world war to a new Cold War. It was an era of reversals, when an old enemy, Germany, was split in two. West Germany became an ally, and our old ally, Russia, the new enemy. It was a time of brinkmanship and egos, a time of fierce determination, of ideology and idealism, and sadly, of foolish naïveté.

This is the world of Jack and Walker in *The Good Man.*

In August of 1945, President Truman empowered two agencies, the Joint Intelligence Objectives Agency (JIOA) and the Office of Strategic Services (OSS) to gather intelligence on the state of German technology and recruit resources for the Cold War against the Soviets. While Operation Overcast, later renamed Paperclip, was initially leaked in 1946, the JIOA would continue to violate Truman's directive to exclude any scientist with a militant Nazi past when it created fictitious biographies for the recruited scientists to work in the US. The name Paperclip came from the paperclips used to attach phony records to the files of former Nazis. Readers who enjoy history and nonfiction can find numerous publications on that secret program at their bookstore or library.

The JIOA disbanded in 1962. The OSS ceased operations in September 1945, but was later reborn as the CIA in September 1947. Operation Paperclip would still have legs as late as 1990.

The Good Man mentions a rare coin, the Constantine Ruble. Eight such coins are known to have existed. The last auction of a Constantine Ruble took place in 2004, and the coin was sold for $525,000. Three original Constantine Rubles are housed at the Hermitage in Russia, and the Smithsonian Institution in the United States.

While *The Good Man* borrows from history, I improvised on events for the sake of telling a tale. Graham Greene did it with his *The Quiet American*. John le Carré's career in British intelligence informs his numerous works. Several of Joseph Kanon's historical thrillers dance around the periphery of historical events. John Banville's *The Untouchable* is a psychological examination of the Soviet spy Anthony Blunt of the Cambridge Five spy ring. Intimations that British-turned-Soviet spies were afoot had begun as early as 1949 when the FBI intercepted telegraph messages from the British Embassy in Washington, DC, to Moscow. It is in this milieu of shady allegiances and motivations that Meeks makes his appearance.

The initial disappearance and later defection of both Guy Burgess and Donald Maclean to the Soviet Union in 1951 confirmed suspicions that a British element had leaked American atomic capability to the Soviets. Allegations that there were Communists within the US government from Senator Joseph McCarthy came as early as February of 1950, and set the stage for the subsequent Red Scare and the executions of the Rosenbergs in 1953.

The last historical borrowing that I must acknowledge is the most neglected, possibly the most obscure to readers, and the most controversial to those conversant with Holocaust history. The character Sheldon is described as a former Sonderkommando. This term is not to be confused with the SS-Sonderkommando Dirlewanger, which was the name for the SS unit directed against Poles and Russians. The Sonderkommandos I allude to were men drawn from prisoners at Auschwitz to facilitate Nazi genocide. These Sonderkommandos themselves were routinely exterminated to prevent any trace evidence of the Final Solution. Lesser known is that Auschwitz did experience a prisoner and Sonderkommando revolt and an especially brutal SS reprisal in October 1944.

The Sonderkommandos were despised, often seen as collaborators by other prisoners in the concentration camps. Few survived the war and shame and survivor's guilt contributed to suppressing the historical record of a terrorized minority. There had been scant mention of Sonderkommandos in Holocaust literature until recently. Testimonies were sporadic, though they had been collected after the war. Since then, times have changed. Shlomo Venezia, a Sonderkommando himself, wrote *Inside the Gas Chambers: Eight Months in the Sonderkommando of Auschwitz*, published in 2011. Venezia, an Italian-Jew, provided consultation and inspiration to Roberto Benigni's film, *Life is Beautiful*. He died in 2012.

The Holocaust Museum and Yad Vashem, the World Holocaust Remembrance Center, recognize the Sonderkommandos as true victims of the Holocaust. Both organizations have collected, documented, and displayed testimonies from Sonderkommandos who survived the Shoah and lived with unspeakable guilt and horrors.

In researching Vienna, past and present, I consulted Paul Hoffmann's *The Viennese: Splendor, Twilight, and Exile*. For those interested in independent Jewish reprisals against Nazi war criminals after World War II and well into the Seventies, I would direct readers to Michael Elkins's *Forged in Fury*.

Fiction makes palpable the recurring nightmares of history.

Acknowledgements

I'm grateful to my publisher, Level Best Books, for their continued faith in my work. Thank you, Dames of Detection.

Hugs and friendship for Shawn Reilly Simmons, my editor.

I'm thankful for the generosity and feedback from my proofreaders Dean Hunt and continuity editor Deb Well. I'm especially thankful to fellow author Tina deBellegarde who proofread the manuscript.

As always, nothing but gratitude to my fellow Level Best authors, and to friends of the pen and keyboard in crime fiction, the best and most supportive community around for a writer.

About the Author

Gabriel Valjan is a member of ITW, MWA, and a lifetime member of Sisters in Crime. He is the author of The Company Files and the Shane Cleary Mysteries with Level Best Books. His work has been nominated for the Agatha, Anthony, Derringer, Shamus, and the Silver Falchion awards. Gabriel received the 2021 Macavity Award for Best Short Story. He is a regular contributor to the blog *Criminal Minds* and an active supporter of writers on social media. Gabriel lives in Boston, and answers to a tuxedo cat named Munchkin.

SOCIAL MEDIA HANDLES:
https://twitter.com/GValjan
https://www.facebook.com/profile.php?id=100011325634871
https://www.instagram.com/gabrielvaljan

AUTHOR WEBSITE:
gabrielvaljan.com

Also by Gabriel Valjan

Shane Cleary Mystery Series
Liar's Dice
Hush Hush
Symphony Road
Dirty Old Town

Company Files Series
The Devil's Music
The Naming Game
The Good Man

www.ingramcontent.com/pod-product-compliance
Lightning Source LLC
Chambersburg PA
CBHW020634110726
47899CB00002B/770